JOY STREET

RUSS BUBAS

Merrimack Media
Cambridge, Massachusetts

Library of Congress Control Number: 2014937370

ISBN: print: 978-1-939166-43-2
ISBN: ebook: 978-1-939166-44-9

This book was printed in the United States of America

Published by Merrimack Media, Cambridge, Massachusetts
April, 2014

Chapter 1

The Landing Zone Bar sat outside the Miami Airport, sharing space on the highway leading in with used car lots, discount rentals and a strip bar. They tried to paint it a Miami Dolphins orange, but it turned out a dark, peeling mustard, as it baked in the unrelenting sun. It was a squat cinder block building square and windowless, except for a high narrow window that advertised Coors Beer next to the formidable front door. A large air conditioner, dripping and oxidized, stuck out through the wall on the side. Walking in from outside, the dark, dank interior caused temporary blindness. People would stop in their tracks, the smell of old beer and wet socks striking them before their vision adjusted.

Inside, Jorge Hornez, called el Horse because of his impressive equipment, sat at the end of the bar sipping his second Patron. At three o'clock on a Monday, he and the bartender were the only two people in the room. The air conditioner pulsed on, working hard and pretty much failing. As Hornez was about to throw down his tequila, a flash of light came from the door. It was quickly muted by the bulk of Eddie Ciracero. Once a boxer, he was now loose and fat, and his thinning hair unsuccessfully tried to cover his large head with an obvious comb over. Letting the door close behind him, he stood looking like a juke box with feet until he could discern Hornez twenty feet away. The bartender picked up a tray of glasses and walked into the back room.

"Horseman." Ciracero yelled as he shuffled down the bar and plopped onto a stool next to Hornez. "How you doin, man?"

"Hanging in there." Hornez replied.

"Yeah, I hear from the putas you are really hanging." Cicacero chuckled at his attempt at humor. He reached over and picked up Hornez's glass, grinned at him and chugged down what was left in it.

"How you doing, Eddie? Still driving the Bentley?" Homez slid his now empty glass back for more.

"Got the sucker right outside. Love that ride."

"Eddie, who the fuck parks a three hundred thousand dollar silver convertible outside the LZ? You want a couple of cops to stick their noses in here to see what's going on?"

"Shit, man, this is Miami. The cops that would look in here would be driving Bentleys themselves. Besides, I'm only here to give you directions. Where the fuck is the bartender?"

"Billy," Hornez yelled, and the bartender appeared from the back. "Give my grandfather and me a couple more shooters." The rocks glasses were quickly topped off and the bartender receded into the back room again.

Ciracero waited until he couldn't see the bartender, downed half of his drink and turned serious. "So, what the fuck? We meeting your guys or not?"

Hornez replied, "They're not my guys. I just happen to know a couple."

"Who you shittin? I hear broads all over talking about the horse. You sure as hell don't get them on your own."

"A couple of parties don't make me a relative. But, yeah, they will meet and talk about a deal. What happens is up to you and them. I just do the intros."

"OK, let's do it. We're ready to go. We can move some heavy cash." He scratched his sagging balloon of a stomach.

"Eddie, I know you, but I don't know who you're in bed with. I don't want to get into a situation where someone shoots the messenger." Hornez tossed down his tequila and tapped the glass on the bar for more. Ciracero paused until the bartender reappeared and refilled the glasses once again.

"I only run with stand-up guys. And, I get a finder's fee. Three percent. I can take care of you. I need you guys to understand that I do nothing in this except the intros. These guys don't fuck around. You want to do a deal, they'll listen. I party sometimes, but I don't know much and I try to stay that way. Your guys understand who they're dealing with?"

"My people are bigger than them. We'll do a deal as long as the product and price is right. You vouch for us and you vouch for them and we do the deal. You walk away with your pockets full and stay away."

"OK. They are going to be hanging out at the Airport Marriott pool bar later today. They're there almost every day. If you want an intro, get over there around five o'clock. I'll do the intros and walk away. You guys do want you want." Hornez fidgeted with a plastic stirrer and took a sip of his tequila.

"What's with the Marriott pool bar? Not exactly quiet."

"They like it because there is a Cuban whorehouse a nine iron shot away. Quiffs in there about 15 years old and can suck the rust off a trailer hitch."

Ciracero laughed. "I like it. Maybe we can celebrate if we do this deal."

Hornez looked around and saw no one, including Billy the bartender. He lowered his voice, "How much you guys lookin for?"

Ciracero's face turned to hard lead, his voice was gravel under a blanket. "You don't need to know any details. You're just the messenger boy."

"Sorry, Eddie. No offense, I was just. . . ."Ciracero's raised hand cut him off. A satisfied grin moved over his sagging face. Still in hushed whispers he bragged, "Between you and me, horse-boy. New York's got maybe five mil to do this if your boys cooperate."

"Holy, shit."

"Yeah, holy shit."

Looking at his watch, Hornez said, "It's a little after three. I'll head over and wait for everyone to show up."

Ciracero kept his grin. "Fuck you. You're riding with me. I don't want you out of my sight until my boys say you can go." Still with a lizard smile, he said, "Besides, you'll like riding in the gray ghost. It rides like a cloud, smooth as Spanish diarrhea."

They finished their drinks and Ciracero led them out the door and into the Bentley. Hornez climbed into the passenger seat as Ciracero was squeezing behind the wheel. He saw the butt of nine millimeter sticking out of Ciracero's boot. The ride was silent, Ciracero whistling softly to himself. The car did ride like a dream.

Chapter 2

Hughes, through a scotch haze, was startled to see the moon through the window behind the bar. It made him realize how long he had been pounding them down while hitting on the nicely racked blonde standing next to him. She stifled a yawn and looked away, tiring of him. Even with a foggy head, Hughes knew this. But with determination fueled by his outrageous bar bill, he decided to give it one more try.

"Like to see my plaze?" He realized it didn't come out right and winced. She looked sadly at him, picked up her gin and tonic, and walked away without another word, leaving him to pay for her three drinks along with his five Dewar's.

He looked down the three deep bar in the seafood restaurant which appeared to be selling more cocktails than seafood. Faneuil Hall attracted young city professionals, along with a hungry herd of suburbanites looking to make someone, or at least the scene. Hughes usually could figure out who was who, but this night, tired and woozy from drink, he was lost in the pagan action.

Out of the corner of his eye, he saw a large guy in a Globe Gym t-shirt staring intently at him. Trying on focus,

Hughes felt a menace growing in him as he realized the guy was someone he had caught stealing, and it had resulted in a swift and ugly termination. He felt a churning in his stomach and figured this was a good time to end the night. Confrontation seemed close and Hughes was in no shape to counter any problems. He tossed his American Express card that read "Hughes Investigations" on the bar, hoping it would not be declined. It still was alive so he left a nice tip and made his way through the crowd, putting a group of giggling women between him and the potential for trouble as he moved outside into the summer night.

It was damp and hazy and the light breeze felt like warm silk on his face. Taking a deep breath and shaking off some of the booze, he stopped, wondering where he had parked the Miata. Getting his bearings, he checked out two blondes in very short skirts walking by arm in arm. Finally figuring out the right direction, he headed down the street and found his blue sports car where he had parked it four hours ago. It now sported a bright orange parking ticket under the wiper. He tossed it into the glove box with four others and headed to Beacon Hill.

Ten minutes of top down air helped clear his head and he found a parking spot on Mt. Vernon, luckily only around the corner from his place. He pulled the top up and locked the car, wincing at the long scratch someone had engineered with a key. The street was empty and dark. At his building, he climbed up the three flights to his one bedroom apartment, tossed his jacket on the couch and stumbled into the bedroom. Just barely getting his clothes off, he hit the bed and fell asleep immediately.

The buzzing came from a distance, getting louder and louder until he realized it was from the front door. Slowly regaining consciousness, through blurred eyes he read the clock on his nightstand: two thirty. Streetlights split the dark of Joy Street, so he knew it was not day. He groaned. Pulling open the drawer on the night stand, he took out the Air Weight .38, and headed into the living room. The outside streetlights lit the room with a soft glow as he made his way to the front window and peered down to the street. He smiled when he recognized the jet-black hair on the top of Angie's head. He buzzed her in, and opened the door a crack, returning the gun to the nightstand. He flopped down on the couch and waited. Angie came in startlingly awake, beautiful, and still in her waitress uniform.

"Christ, Dan, if you give me a key, I won't have to wake you," she said, going right to the kitchen and pouring a glass of water for herself.

"Hi to you too. Nice to see you. Roommate problems again?"

She took a sip of water. "Rachel's got that scumbag over again. I can't stand that guy and I can't stand their moaning. Can I crash here again?"

"Sure, I'm still asleep, so come to bed when you want," He got up and headed back to the bedroom, forgetting he was nude. Angie watched his white bottom disappear into the bedroom then she slipped off her blouse and skirt, tossed her bra aside and followed him in. Something woke Hughes up in the middle of the night. Soft focus light filtered in from the street. Angie was quietly asleep and he watched her for minutes. He realized that, besides her sensuous beauty, she had a deep and solid goodness about her. He snuggled in, spooning her and drifted back into a dreamless sleep.

Yelling outside and the crash of garbage cans being tossed to the sidewalk woke Hughes. Morning sunlight streamed in. The noise and the light hurt his head. After a moment, he realized he couldn't feel his left arm and finally figured out Angie was lying on it. When he pulled it out from under her, she woke and smiled at him.

"Morning."

"Good morning. I had this fabulous dream last night that this incredible hot blooded Mediterranean woman came in and screwed me to death."

Angie stretched. "You always have weird dreams when you drink too much. No respectable Mediterranean woman would go anywhere near you."

"You're right, it would have to be a pack of them to handle me. What time is it?"

"It's time for coffee. I'll make it." Angie got up and ambled over to the front window, giggled and waved to the garbage men outside. "I think I made their day," she said, heading into the kitchen.

Hughes watched her walk by, her breasts high and pink tipped. "Been trimming the bush again I see," he said.

Over her shoulder she said, "You'd get lost in it if I didn't."

He wondered again why he chased others. It was probably the chase rather than the kill.

He tried to will the throbbing in his head away. Angie was banging around in the kitchen. He lurched out of bed and took a look. She was standing in front of the stove wearing only an apron around her waist. Coffee was dripping while she was swirled eggs around in a pan.

Hughes smiled. "Every man's fantasy–a beautiful brunette cooking in the nude for him."

"Don't get used to it, I just don't want to get spots on my uniform. Maybe you can someday think about getting a washer and dryer in this joint." She said, not turning around.

"Still, I like your outfit. Maybe you should stay this way." He reached around her waist and nuzzled the back of her neck. Angie squealed and pulled away halfheartedly.

"The eggs are almost done. Get some pants on and butter the toast. If you think we're eating in the nude, you're crazy."

Within minutes, Angie had the tiny table set with mismatched plates. She divided up the scrambled eggs and poured two cups of coffee. Hughes pulled on jeans and a Red Sox t-shirt and grinned at Angie, who was now wearing her bra, bikini panties and a blouse. They ate in silence as Hughes' headache melted away.

Finishing, they rinsed the dishes together. Hughes felt he would live after all. "Been invited to a cookout Saturday after next at Bill Halloran's house. Coming with me?" Hughes asked, as he poured another cup of coffee for himself.

"Bill Halloran? Where is that, the burbs?"

"Yeah, Bill my FBI friend. They live on the South Shore."

"God, it sounds dreadful. Men standing around with beers watching hot dogs burn on a grill, while the women work their asses off setting up and cleaning up. Isn't she the perfect wife? She took her apron off and tossed it aside. Do you have to go?" she asked.

"Come on, Angie. It's Americana. How can we survive against the terrorists if we're not filled with greasy burgers washed down with cold beer? It's what makes us strong. And, yes, she does seem to be perfect."

"I'm sure I have to work all next weekend."

"It's not a forced march, but it's good for me to have a

contact with the Bureau. Bill's a good guy and can do me some favors. I think you'll have a good time."

"OK, I'll see if it works, but if the Stepford wife says anything about my tight jeans, it's you that will pay," she said as she headed for the shower.

She came out twenty minutes later, hair still wet and glistening, now redressed in her waitress white blouse and black skirt. Hughes looked up from the bar spotting report he was writing to marvel how she could look so good in so many ways.

"I'm bartending tonight, five to closing. Stopping by?" she asked.

"Doubt it. I've got a worker's comp fraud surveillance to do and I have to be in Worcester by five o'clock in the morning. Got to leave by four to get there. Early to bed and early to rise, as they say."

She was quiet for a minute. "Well, let me know. I guess I'll see you when I see you." She headed for the door. With her hand on the doorknob, she stopped and turned halfway around. "Danny?"

"Yeah?" he said, still tapping on his laptop.

"What's with us?" she asked quietly.

"What do you mean?" he said, engrossed and not looking up.

"Nothing. See you later." She left, closing the door softly behind her.

Chapter 3

I t was still dark when Hughes pulled himself out of bed. He was a night person and hated early mornings. By the time he threw the binoculars, tape recorder and two bottles of water into his gear bag and headed the Miata out onto the Mass Pike, the sun was rising behind him. It was a shimmering orange platter, predicting a steamy day ahead. Getting off at the Worcester exit, he followed the directions he had gleaned from MapQuest. Stopping briefly at a drive-thru Dunkin Donuts for a large black coffee and a breakfast sandwich, he smoothly shifted the small car along back roads. It was just before five and he finally felt awake when he found his destination.

The white clapboard house was set back a distance from the road. Its peeling paint looked like a bad case of acne. A blue Ford F-150 pickup truck with a dent in the rear right fender was parked in the driveway. There was no sign of life. The subject, a guy by the name of Bobby (AKA Bucky) Merrick supposedly hurt his back picking up a case of beer at the distributor where he worked. He'd been collecting worker's compensation for five months. Every attempt to determine if and how badly he was hurt had been met with lame excuses. The company believed he was not really hurt and was working someplace else. Hughes had been hired to find this out. Because Merrick was represented by counsel, Hughes couldn't just ask where he was working, something he had done in the past. Surveillance was the only way and Hughes knew he had to be lucky as well as good. The license plate on the truck verified it belonged to Bucky.

Hughes did two drive-bys, looking for the best static surveillance spot. The truck, if it left with Bucky, could go either left or right. If the Miata was parked on the wrong side, the truck would drive right by him and he could easily be made. And, parked in the wrong spot could create a confrontation with a suspicious neighbor which would blow the surveillance. There was little traffic and few places to park the Miata. These surveillances always seemed to be difficult. It was most likely that the truck, if it left, would head out to the left and toward the main road. So Hughes finally found a place to park a good two hundred yards away from the house in a shallow turnaround. He scrunched down as much as was possible for a two hundred pound guy in a small car and waited, sipping the now tepid coffee. He couldn't see the house, but the driveway was in a direct line of sight and the truck leaving should be obvious. But he knew how fast that could happen and knew he had to concentrate. Boredom was the big enemy of this work. Hardly any cars had passed and, so far, no one seemed to notice him. Almost two hours passed when he saw the truck come bouncing backwards out of the driveway and speed away from him. Hughes tossed the coffee cup aside, splashing what was left onto the passenger seat, started the car and pushed the gear shift hard forward. The truck, presumably with Bucky at the wheel, was already gaining speed.

"Shit." Hughes muttered under his breath as he missed second gear and the truck made a hard right turn and went out of sight. The Miata sped to the corner, the engine whining at the high revolutions. Stopping hard to let a Buick go by, Hughes pulled out and exhaled as he saw the truck ahead. Using the Buick as cover, he went into a more relaxed surveillance mode, keeping the fat lumbering car between him and the truck. The F-150 rumbled along at the speed limit, and Hughes figured it was heading for I-290. It cleared a traffic light just as it was turning red and the Buick in front stopped for the light. Hughes brought the sports car to the side and saw the truck getting away from him. Disregarding the horn of an oncoming Lexus, he slammed into first and yanked the little car around the Buick, running the light, his tires squealing. Sure enough, up ahead, the Ford pulled onto the entrance ramp for the interstate heading north. The small engine of the Miata screamed but he was able to keep the truck in sight, hopefully unnoticed by its driver. After fifteen minutes, it moved to the right and slowed slightly. Hughes sought cover behind a swaying SUV, and then swiftly cut over when Bucky swung onto an off ramp. Out of the corner of his eye, he saw the SUV swerve as he cut it off.

The F-150 rounded off the exit ramp and onto a two-lane road littered with rundown frame houses, used car lots and bars. Population thinned as the truck continued along, making a left onto an even narrower road, and moving at a fast pace. Hughes had to drop back so as to not get seen and now he could glimpse the truck only occasionally when the road straightened.

Up ahead, the truck made a series of turns, and Hughes had to up and downshift maniacally to keep pace at a distance. Finally, the truck turned into a dirt driveway. Driving past he looked straight ahead, trying to see out of his peripheral vision. It was a new house of sizable dimensions and appeared to be under construction. There were two trucks and a car parked on the property next to a pile of lumber. A large man in coveralls was standing at the side of the house watching the F-150 pull in. As Hughes went by, he saw the man move toward the driver's door.

A quarter mile down the road, Hughes made a hard three-point turn and headed back, again looking by not looking. No one seemed to notice him. He saw a hulking figure he decided must be Bucky talking to two other men in work clothes. Hughes found a dirt road a short distance away and pulled in. He jumped out of the car, taking his miniature video camera and a Red Sox cap. He pulled the cap down low on his head, held the camera alongside his leg, and he strolled toward the property hoping he looked like a neighbor taking a walk. *I need a dog to pull this off,* he thought to himself.

He ambled past on the opposite side of the road, and saw the previously described Bucky carrying an armload of two-by-fours to the side of the house. *Gotcha!* Pausing briefly he brought the camera to hip level, glanced down into the view finder and shot a good two minutes of the allegedly disabled Bucky, cigarette dangling from his mouth, carrying heavy loads of building materials back and forth from the lumber pile to the house.

Hughes walked farther up the road and out of sight of the property. After a bit he turned around and headed back. This time he kept the camera going the whole time he walked past, catching a panorama of the site and the beehive of activity, and a few more action shots of Bucky. It didn't matter if he was noticed now, unless Bucky figured out what he was doing and had thoughts of homicide. Hughes got back to the car and drove to the property, this time stopping directly in front to shoot another minute or two from the car. This time the workers did notice him and he saw one of them say something to Bucky. But within seconds he was gone, driving away fast, smiling to himself, video camera tucked safely behind the seat. He made a hard left, then right and pulled into a driveway and waited. No suspicious cars went by and Hughes was content no one was following. He swung out, doubled back and decided he would treat himself to a real breakfast at the next welcoming diner.

Chapter 4

The sun was high and hot when he finished his breakfast and ambled out to the Miata. With the video safely tucked away, he figured Bucky was appropriately screwed. He planned to spend the rest of the day writing up the report and invoice to the insurance company. Maybe he would call Angie. He had a lot of paperwork to get caught up, some back report supplements and bills to pay, but he had little interest in sitting down at the rickety desk he used as a home office. He was almost to the Allston tolls when his cell phone rang.

"Hi, this is Dan."

"Captain Dan, what's happening?" He recognized Bill Halloran's voice immediately and checked the time on his dashboard to figure out if he was on or off the clock.

"Just finished a worker's comp surveillance and going back to bed."

"No can do, amigo. Meet me at O'Malley's around four and we'll figure out our next adventure." Dan figured Bill was on and also off the clock–paid for a full day but actually working far less. Good thing criminals didn't know the Bureau was mostly on cruise control. Dan found a parking spot on the back side of Beacon Hill and stowed his gear and video upstairs. Checking his watch, he figured there was no time for the paperwork, or Angie, so he grabbed his nylon gear bag, stuffed new shorts and a t-shirt in it and headed over to LA Sports. The club was an expensive luxury he kept telling himself he couldn't afford, but he needed the workouts and the eye candy was exceptional. Every time he got bored and headed for the lockers, he would spot another woman showing off a fabulous body, and do another set of reps. Kept him in shape and happy. This day was no different and he killed a good part of the afternoon working out. He showered and shaved in the club, sat in the steam for twenty minutes and got himself feeling as good as he could get. Refreshed and squeaky clean, he was at O'Malley's just before four. Coming in from the shimmering glare of the day to the cave cool dark of the bar, it took him a minute to adjust. The décor was shiny dark oak, faux tiffany lights and red vinyl barstools. Dan squinted before he spotted Bill and the white shirt and narrow dark tie of another agent. Dan could tell they had been there for some time.

"Capitano," Bill yelled over as he spotted Hughes. He waved him over and Hughes took a barstool next to him. He nodded to the bartender and asked for a Sam Summer draft, which arrived almost immediately.

"Dan, this is Pat Bailey," Bill said, introducing his colleague. Dan reached across to shake hands and settled back to take a sip of his beer. The glass was icy cold and the beer deliciously sweet and tart at the same time. Bailey had his jacket off and over the back of the barstool. His tie was loosened and his white shirt was untucked, no doubt covering his Sig. Bill was in a polo shirt that read "Molson's Beer" over a picture of a moose wearing a pair of jeans.

Being on the surveillance squad, Bill worked less than anyone Hughes knew.

"What's happening?" Dan asked.

"Hanging out until the bright light fades. I hear there's a small party of flight attendants in East Boston later. Will Angie let you out?" Bill was a big man, including his face, which was usually lit up by his smile, as it was now.

"No plans. I'll see what happens." Dan was always wary of Bill's parties because he could never keep up with the level of alcohol Bill drained without regard to type or quantity.

"Pat's on the OC squad. Give him one of your cards."

Dan fished in his wallet, found a crinkled business card and passed it over to Bailey.

"You do anything with narcotics?" he asked.

"Once in a while. Depends who's involved." Bailey finished his beer and signaled for another. When the bartender served it, Bill ordered a scotch, which was placed next to the beer he was drinking.

"I once had an undercover at the airport and he found they were bringing drugs up from Miami in the food carts. I called the Bureau and said I had a good case for them. A couple of guys came over, listened to me for a while and said they were only interested in kingpin cases. Four kilos a flight and they thought it wasn't worth their time."

"Yeah." Bailey said. "We get particular sometimes. What did you do?"

"The staties took it and did a nice bust. My guy got pulled in with the bad guys. In the front door and out the back," Dan said. Bailey smiled.

Bill finished his scotch and ordered another. Some workers started to drift in early, including two secretary types who sat at a high top by the window. Bill checked them out with a predatory eye. After a couple of minutes, he waved them over to the bar. One was wearing practical shoes and a dress that did not quite hide unfortunate hips. The other, a blonde with bangs, wore a scoop neck top that showed an interesting pattern of freckles. Dan started to feel more invigorated.

The summer day eased unnoticed into a sultry and glowing evening. Bill had two more scotches to match the Margaritas the girls drank. Dan coasted with a couple of gin and tonics. There was a lot of laughing and talking over one another. Pat said he had to head home to Framingham, mumbling something about traffic and having to go to a soccer game. Shortly after he left, scoop neck bent over to pull something from her purse, letting Dan know where the freckles stopped and the cream began. By eight o'clock, a plate of nachos and a few more drinks later, both women said they thought the party in East Boston was an interesting idea. Bill had a car he confiscated from a narc parked in the Bureau garage and left to get it. Dan tossed his American Express card on the bar, wincing over the numbers on the slip. Bill pulled up outside and the two couples piled into the black Caddie. In East Boston, Bill got lost looking for the party and was driving aimlessly through the tight streets of the neighborhood, while Dan and the blonde cuddled in the cavernous back seat. He had his arm around her and she nestled into his side. Before he knew it she had reached inside his pants and was going down on him. Bill grinned in the rearview mirror. After several minutes, Dan sobered up a little and lost interest in the party, and in the blonde. He remembered he had promised to call Angie and felt a small tinge of guilt.

"Bill, I just remembered, I've got to get back on a commitment. Can you drop me off near my place?"

The blonde looked at him through hazy, angry eyes. She pulled back and pulled her skirt down. "What? Finished partying?" she asked, her voice as brittle as a plastic fork.

"Sorry, forgot. Really important. I'll call tomorrow and we can find something to do."

Bill was slowing down as well and seemed perfectly content to close the night. With an affirmative grunt, he turned the heavy car around and headed back through the tunnel, dropping Dan off at the foot of Beacon Street. The blonde stared stoically straight ahead when he tried to give her a kiss on her cheek. Bill said he would drop the girls off, and he headed down Tremont Street. Hughes made his way up the hill, clomped up the two flights to his place, shed his clothes and hit the bed exhausted.

Chapter 5

Hughes woke with the low throb of a headache and tried to remember the last sixteen hours. Then he remembered Angie and wondered if he really did not call her like he had promised. *Got to mend that fence.* As his cranial cleared, he tried to figure out what he had to do this day. He realized not much. There were a couple of bar spots he could do which would generate a couple of hundred bucks of billing, but those jobs were at night. He went out and searched the kitchen for something to calm the agitation in his stomach. He found half a loaf of rye bread from Panera, some week old cream cheese and half a bag of Dunkin Donuts coffee. He ground the coffee and made a pot, toasting the bread and spreading it with the cream cheese, as the coffee brewed. Two cups and a cream cheese sandwich later, he figured he would live.

He stuffed his bag with clean workout gear, threw on jeans, running shoes and a sweatshirt with the sleeves cut off, and headed across the common to LA Sports. After an hour and a half of pushing weights and ogling the secretaries on break, he began to feel like he would make it to nightfall. After a steam and a chat with the towel guy about who of any importance was new to the club, he got back to the apartment and, with a lot of effort, forced himself to sit at his desk and attack the business going stale there.

After two hours and another cup of coffee thick as tar, he felt clear enough to call
Angie. It was like opening a door to a refrigerator.

"Hi, Ang, how's everything?"

"Fine" She knifed the word off. He suddenly realized how important she was to him and tried to scramble to get back on track.

"How about we get away this weekend? Maybe head over to the Vineyard or someplace to get out of the city?" he said spontaneously.

There was silence for a minute. "I'm on the schedule for Saturday."

"Can you book off? I heard the weather is going to be great.

More silence. Then, "I'll try and let you know." She hung up without another word.

Hughes went to his bathroom, found some aspirin next to the toothpaste, took two, and sat back down at his desk. He thought for a minute, then called the Steamship Authority and got the schedule. He checked the balance on his Visa card and figured he could do a day or two at the Harbor View. He then looked at his list of things to do and found that he had a couple of bar spots he could get to and make maybe enough for dinners and drinks on a getaway.

An hour and a half later, the reports were finished and a couple of bills were ready for the mail. Given the state of his hangover, Hughes felt this was a major accomplishment.

A warm and glowing summer evening was descending. He threw on a black t-shirt, tan slacks and a tan natural shoulder jacket. He slipped a small Sony digital recorder in the inner pocket of the jacket, and tucked a small pad and a pencil, shortened to one inch, in his pants pocket and headed out. The first bar was in a large motel tucked in among shopping malls in the western suburbs. The Miata hit the turnpike at a good speed and he was there in twenty-five minutes.

The Noir Bar was appropriately dark. Hughes let his eyes adjust and made out a couple and one guy at the bar and a smattering of people at tables. He quickly scoped out where the register was located and where the tip cup sat, and found a seat with a clear line of sight to both. One bartender was on duty. He wore slicked back hair and had a small tuft of hair between his lip and chin. He was leaning over the service bar whispering to a cocktail waitress with hair the color of brass and vivid red fingernails. It took him three to four minutes before he realized he had another customer at the bar. Hughes was seemingly intent on watching the baseball game on the television hanging over the end of the bar, and acted mildly surprised when the bartender finally approached. He gave a practiced smile and a nod to Hughes.

"How about a Dewar's on the rocks," Hughes ordered.

"Coming right up." The bartender was big and burly, squarely built. He free poured while Hughes counted out the seconds. After four full seconds the rocks glass was filled to the brim with the golden liquid and ice. The bartender placed the glass down on a clean paper cocktail napkin and shoved a half filled bowl of peanuts towards Hughes before turning back to the waitress waiting at the service bar. Hughes made a mental note of it all. While still staring at the Red Sox game, he reached into his pocket and extracted a twenty dollar bill, which he placed on the bar. It sat there for several minutes while Hughes appeared engrossed in the game, munching on the nuts and sipping the scotch slowly. A couple of minutes later, the bartender noticed the twenty, collected it and rang up the sale on the cash register. He placed eleven dollars in change back on the bar in front of Hughes. Hughes chose not to notice.

The bar got busier as Hughes pretended to watch the game. A couple arrived and sat on the opposite side of the bar. A guy came in and sat a few stools down from Hughes. He watched as the bartender issued a check to the couple for their cosmopolitan and martini, and the guy near Hughes tossed a bill on the bar for his beer. At about that same time, Hughes gestured to the bartender for a repeat scotch. While staring at the TV, Hughes watched the bartender collect the money for the beer, then pick up the ten off the bar for Hughes's second scotch. The bartender's hands were fast, but Hughes followed his recordings with the register. He saw $5.50 in the LED window. After a quick move to the tip cup next to the register, the bartender turned and dumped some change in front of one of the customers and then placed a dollar in front of Hughes. Nothing was rung up on the register for Hughes's second drink. Hughes was pretty sure the ten dollar bill that he had marked with an infrared crayon ended up in the tip cup. *Gotcha!*

While sipping the second scotch, Hughes got a chance to chat with the bartender. "Sox don't suck as much this year," he said, by way of an opening.

"But they'll still break your heart," the bartender replied. Hughes saw his nametag said Bill.

Hughes smiled. "You know, I was in here a couple of weeks ago, I forget which day, but I got lucky. Doesn't look like much around tonight."

"If you got lucky in here, you got lucky. Mostly salesmen and sometimes blouzers. But if you wait until around closing, you might trip over something.

"Ok, I'll hang out a little. How about another Dewar's?"

"Sure." He walked off and poured a scotch with ice to the brim of a tall glass.

Placing the drink down on a paper napkin, Bill gave a little wink to Hughes. "It's on me," he said in a low voice.

"Thanks." Hughes tossed a five on the bar, a grateful tip for the free drink. The bartender skimmed it off the bar and tossed it into his tip cup. When the bartender headed back to the service bar, Hughes brought the glass to the edge of the bar and slowly poured most of it out on the worn turquoise rug. He took a small sip of the remainder and slid off the barstool, giving a wave to the bartender who barely noticed.

Hughes moved into the lobby and sat on a couch. He glanced around to make sure no one was paying any attention to him as he dialed the number of the general manager's mobile phone. It was answered on the third ring.

"Danny Hughes here. I was just in the bar and your guy Bill has a ten dollar bill in his tip cup that belongs to you."

"Jesus, you sure?"

"As sure as I can be and, because he likes me so much, he gave me a freebie. Strong enough to take the rust off my car bumper."

"I had a feeling I couldn't trust that guy," Grant, the manager, said.

"Want me to have a little chat with him? At the rate he's going, I figure about a hundred a shift, not counting what he pushes without charge to build his tips."

"Yeah, I have to move on this guy. My beverage costs

are out of sight. I'll get the assistant manager to fill in for him. How do you want to do it?"

"I'll come to your office, then you can bring him in."

"Ok, do you know where I am?"

"Behind the front desk?"

"Come on back."

Grant Levy was a comer. He was young, wore narrow Italian suits like he was born in them and ran the hotel efficiently, while seemingly completely relaxed. He could be running a five star in Hong Kong, or somewhere like that, in a couple of years. His office was small and sparse. The desk was clean except for his computer and a photo of a very attractive blonde sitting someplace tropical. The shelf behind the desk was a series of neatly stacked papers arranged in a row. Grant got up from his desk, flashed a dazzling smile and stuck his hand out.

"Danny, how've you been?"

"Great. You know how it is. Every day is a holiday, every night's a party."

"Yep, we are living the good life," he said with just an edge of sarcasm. "What have we got here?"

"The bartender in the lobby bar, nametag Bill, is a partner without investment. I figure he's into you for about a hundred a day, more when you're busy."

"Bill Healy. I thought so. Beverage costs are way out of line and that guy is just way too nice to me. Volunteers for every holiday and loves the nightshift. What should we do?"

"Well, I assume he's not going to be on your dance card much longer. Got nothing to lose to have a little chat with him and see if you can get some money back."

Grant flashed his smile. "Let's do it. How do you want to handle it?"

"I need an office that's quiet and I need you to be available. How about this one?"

"You got it. I need to talk with my chef anyway. When you need me, call the front desk and have them page me. What do we do?"

"Just give me five minutes to set the environment up and have your manager bring him back here. Don't say anything to him about what it's about. I need the initiative, so I'll do the intros and explain the facts of life to him."

Grant grinned and headed out the door. "Five minutes. Oh boy."

Hughes arranged the chairs, raising his behind the desk a little and positioning the visitor's chair close to the front of the desk. He frowned over the style of the chair, preferring one without arms to better read body language. He found some file folders on the back shelf and placed them on the desk so they appeared to belong to him. From the narrow black briefcase that he retrieved from his car, he took out a leather bound pad and started jotting notes on it. A minute or two later, the door opened and the room manager let Bill in. Hughes looked at him with empty eyes and thanked the manager, who closed the door behind him.

"Hi, Bill. Remember me?" Hughes said.

Bill was a hulking presence, big all around, but with a sagging gut.

He grumbled. "What's this about?"

Hughes could sense his nervousness and smiled to himself. He held his hand up in reply and said, "Bill, sit down." Hughes gestured to the chair but remained standing behind the desk. Bill sat and Hughes rustled through the papers for a minute in silence. The tension in the room rose like a pressure cooker on high heat.

Hughes sat down and without looking up, said evenly, "Bill, spell your last name for me, and give me your social security number."

Bill complied with it with declining arrogance and Hughes figured he was on first base. He wrote down the information before looking up. He sat up straight and looked at Bill with menacing eyes and arched brows.

In a louder voice he asked, "You on parole or probation?"

Bill was startled by that. He paused and said, "Not anymore."

"What was the problem?" Hughes voice was a little gentler.

"They said I assaulted a guy, but it was in defense."

Hughes paused and wrote some gibberish on his pad. Then, figuring the time was right, he said with resolute command, "Bill, I'm not a police officer and you are not under arrest at this time. I'm a private investigator and I know you have been accepting customer payments and not ringing up some sales but instead keeping the money for yourself." He avoided the word "stealing." "You are in a hell of a jam and I'm the only way you can get out of it." Hughes had the initiative and knew it. Bill still postured defiance, but his shoulders sagged slightly and his eyelids fluttered. He was a big man, but Hughes had the presence. He was in charge.

Hughes continued, "There are two things you have to do to get out of this. Do not, and I stress, do not, lie to me. I will ask you questions most of which I know the answers to, and if I catch you in a lie, all bets are off. The second thing is to demonstrate your sincerity in paying back what you owe."

Bill nodded slightly but said, "I didn't do anything."

Hughes held his hand up again to stop him from saying anything more. "Bill, there is now a marked ten dollar bill in your tip cup. I'm thirty seconds from bagging it as evidence. We've been watching you now for months and know exactly what's been going on," he lied. "You have two choices. You can deal with me, or you can continue to lie and I can recommend the hotel prosecute you for larceny and embezzlement. Doesn't matter to me." Hughes's voice was like grinding stone. He paused. His presence filled the room.

Bill sat motionless. Tiny beads of sweat broke out on his forehead. Before he could say anything, Hughes pushed his initiative.

"Alright, Bill." Hughes said in a lower tone. "You seem like a pretty good guy. If you make a fair effort to pay back what you took, I'll work with you to dodge this bullet."

"I only did it once," Bill said under his breath. Hughes held his hand up again and threw out a bluff. "We've been watching you for the past ten months. At about one hundred dollars a week times forty weeks, that's about four thousand dollars. Will you pay this back?"

There was another slight shaking of his head, this time with resolution. "I don't think it was that much," he said.

"Look, Bill, what's worse, the crime or the cover up? It doesn't matter if you took a hundred dollars or ten thousand dollars, it's still taking someone else's money. Then he threw out a bone. "Look, if you make an honest effort to pay this back, I will ask that your employment records here don't show anything about this so maybe you can get another job."

"Does this mean I'm fired?" Bill asked, stupidly.

Hughes gave him a look that said, "Duh," and immediately started writing out a statement on a pad he pulled out from his folder. In it, Hughes wrote that Bill admitted taking about a hundred dollars a week for about ten months and admitted being responsible for four thousand dollars in theft. (How did he steal $4000? $100 per week for 10 weeks is $1000. Was he stealing other stuff?) He wrote that Bill was sorry he did this and would never steal from the hotel again, and would pay back all that he took. He also wrote that the statement was made of Bill's free will without any threats or promises made to or against him. When Hughes was finished, he had Bill read it, sign it and initial in a couple of places where errors were purposely made. Bill finished signing it and sunk lower in his chair.

Hughes then said, "Do you get along ok with Mr. Levy?"

"I guess so. Never any problems, I think."

"Ok. Here's what's going to happen. I'm going to call him into the office. You tell him what has been going on and tell him you are sorry and will do what you can to pay back the money. Maybe he'll give you a break." Bill looked at him with an empty stare. Hughes called the front desk and asked them to have Levy come back to his office. He then took the statement and told Bill to sit where he was and went out to head him off.

Grant Levy came up in a half run. "What happened?"

"Ok, I got a statement for four thousand dollars. I'm going to have him admit to you as well. You act shocked and listen to his tale of woe for a minute, then suspend him without pay pending further investigation, and give him a week to get the money back. When and if he pays you back, fire him for cause. Follow my lead."

They walked to the office where Bill was sitting with all the arrogance seeped out of him. He looked slightly smaller in size.

Hughes was in charge. "Bill, tell Mr. Levy what's been going on. Remember, whatever you do, do not lie."

Levy stared at Bill. "What the hell is going on?"

Bill hesitated and Hughes said, "Bill?" in a harsh tone.

Bill looked at Levy and it poured out. "I'm sorry, Mr. Levy. I'll never do it again and I'll pay you back."

"Do what again, Bill?" Levy asked and looked to Hughes, standing behind Bill, who winked.

"I've been clipping sales. I only did it when I had to and I'm really sorry. You've been good to me and I've been stupid," his voice cracking.

Hughes, satisfied that a verbal confession was made, jumped in. "Mr. Levy, Bill has been clipping sales at the bar. He says he thinks he took four thousand dollars. I think it was more, but I'll give him the benefit of the doubt if he makes an effort to pay it back."

Bill looked up at Levy with soft boiled eyes and nodded. Levy glared back.

Hughes kept up the pressure. "You could call the police and have
Bill arrested and charged with larceny over and embezzlement. But, maybe he is sincere about paying it back. It's your call."

Levy got it and said, "Bill you let me down. I trusted you. But, if this man thinks you are being honest with us, I won't make any decision right away. You are suspended without pay until I decide what to do." He looked to Hughes for guidance.

Hughes picked it up. "I would not make a decision for two weeks. If Bill comes back within that time and pays back all that he took, maybe you can give him a break. But he's got to make the effort and if he tries to screw you, I'd get the criminal complaint out and get him arrested."

Bill looked at Hughes fearfully. "I don't have four thousand to give back right away. You can take it out of my salary."

"You have no salary from here starting now," said Hughes. "You didn't hesitate to take the money and so you can't take your time to pay it back. Borrow it, mortgage your house, sell your car, we don't care. But you are not to return to this property without permission. If you do, we will consider you a trespasser and have you arrested for that. You can call Mr. Levy no later than two weeks from now and make arrangements to make restitution, otherwise you are in limbo and not welcome." He looked up to Levy and said, "That ok with you?"

"Ok, I'll give him the two weeks." He turned to Bill and asked for his keys.

Hughes said, "Call security and have Bill escorted off the property. Anything he has that belongs to him, he can pick up when he makes restitution."

A young and nervous looking security guard came in within minutes and waited. Hughes told him to hold for a minute then walked out with Bill. He took him aside and said in a soft and polite tone, "Bill, you did some really stupid things here, but you have a chance to make it up and not let it ruin your life. Come back with the money and I think Levy will give you that break."

Bill trembled slightly and stuck out his hand. "Thank you, Mr. Hughes. I appreciate it."

Hughes nodded to the security officer, who then led Bill out the front door, the front desk personnel watching in shock.

Levy watched him leave. He turned to Hughes and said, "Think he'll pay me back?"

"If not, I'll go in and ask for a probable cause hearing

for a criminal complaint to get issued. That will summons him in and get his attention."

"Thanks, Danny. Good job as usual. Can I get you something to eat?"

"Thanks, I'm good, Grant. I would appreciate my invoice getting paid fairly quickly, though."

"No problem." They shook hands and Hughes left, looking in all directions for a busted bartender who may be looking for retaliation. He started the Miata and headed into the night for the next bar.

Chapter 6

The pool area at the Marriott was surprisingly quiet. A pasty family of four was splashing around in the shallow end, while the Cuban bartender gazed sleepily across the empty bar. Ciracero pushed his copious belly up against the bar and ordered two double Patrons on the rocks. Hornez stood next to him, while using his peripheral vision to scope out the area. The bartender eyed them suspiciously, but said nothing as he poured the drinks. Almost on cue, two men emerged from the rear door of the hotel. The older man, about forty, was wearing a light beige linen suit with a white shirt and shiny black tie. He was thin and immaculately groomed with a full head of hair, worn pulled back in a short ponytail. He walked with the sideways grace of a lizard. His younger companion, wearing a white natural shoulder jacket over a black t-shirt, had the bulk and plodding gait of a body builder. There was a strange sexual quality about both.

They sat at a patio table a good distance away from the bar and waited silently. Ciracero looked around and, satisfied what he saw was what it was, ambled over to the table. He grinned broadly.

"Gentlemen. Can I get you something refreshing to

drink?" The two men looked at him with indifference. The older man nodded.

Ciracero went back to the bar and ordered two more double Patrons. He whispered to Hornez, "Come over, but keep your mouth shut." He carried the drinks to the table with Hornez following behind. The two men looked suspiciously at Hornez. Ciracero, picking up on the tension, said, "My man Hornez is with me. He's square. I'll vouch for him. Ok?" The older man, after a cold stare, nodded again.

Ciracero took a sip of his tequila and smiled. "Ok, if you have something to move, we are ready to do business. How about we start with your names?"

"Call me John," the older of the two said. The younger man sat silent.

"Ok, John. My people are looking for good business. We have some depth in our potential investment."

The man called John replied, "What is the so-called depth of your investment." He looked over at Hornez warily.

Ciracero took another deep sip and let the smooth warmth settle. He smiled again. "We have maybe something around three mil, or maybe more."

The two Columbians sat quietly for a moment. Then the younger man said in a whisper, "Bullshit."

John followed up in a soft voice, and spoke in a measured tone. "We know of your people and we do not believe that level of business can be done."

Ciracero grinned. "We have merged. New York and Boston. We have the depth."

The two Columbians looked at each other expressionless. Hornez stiffened slightly. This was something new to him.

John picked up his glass of tequila, looked at the crystal liquid and placed the glass back on the table.

"Maybe it can be done. You talk to your people and be here alone two days from now. We will consider arrangements."

With that the two men stood, bowed slightly and walked away. The younger man, following behind the older man, grinned over his shoulder as they disappeared into the cool dark of the lobby.

"Whew," Ciracero sighed. "Those are some heavy dudes."

"What do you think?" asked Hornez.

"I think we just got a deal. I'll talk to New York; they'll talk to Boston and pull this together. There is maybe six mil riding on this. All we want is the trickle down, hey amigo?"

"You coming back alone?"

"Sure, this is the closing of the deal. No one wants it to fuck up. But I'll make sure one of the boys is close by, just in case."

Hornez shrugged. He drank the last of his drink and settled back in his chair. The family had left unnoticed. He smiled back at Ciracero as he considered what had just happened. They each had another round, Hornez waiting for Ciracero to get itching to speak to his contacts. Ciracero finally said he had some private discussions to make and told Hornez he could get a cab back to wherever he was going. Hornez mildly complained, then got up and walked to the front door where a cab was waiting. He jumped in and gave directions to Hallandale. He stared out the window as the cab followed traffic up A1A, and reached into his pocket to cradle the throwaway phone. A call would be made in the next thirty minutes.

Chapter 7

In Boston, a muggy summer storm moved in, announcing itself with darkening clouds and occasional flashes of lightning. At the FBI offices at Center Plaza, opposite the monolithic City Hall, Bill Halloran sat at his desk, oblivious to the occasional low rumble of thunder outside. As he leafed through the latest intelligence summaries, Pamela, an administrative assistant, sauntered by his office door and he gave her tight backside an approving leer. The phone rang.

"Halloran," he answered.

"It's Sunshine."

Halloran sat up straight and glanced out the door. "You on a secure line?" he asked.

"I'm on a throwaway which will shortly be in the Intercoastal. Got some sweet shit for you. Sitting down?"

"Don't jerk me around. I hope it's not which Miami spic is screwing which Cuban puta again. Earn your money this time."

"Just left a little pow-wow where the boys down here are looking to score big with some Columbian heavies. They're talking in the six mil range."

Halloran paused. "You're shittin me. You better not be

smoking weed again. We don't know of anyone in that league."

Hornez chuckled over the tinny line. "The best part is it's a cooperative deal between New York and Boston. They're merging money for a major score."

"Jesus Christ. Who in Boston?"

"Don't know all the players yet, but my boy is meeting again in two days to set up the deal. I might be able to get more then."

"Sunshine, this may make you the best CI around. Talk to no one but me and get back as soon as you get anything more. This kind of money will bring out the big boys and we can maybe nail a kingpin. Call me on my number two cell. Got that number?"

"Yeah. Got that. Keep that hard-on until I get back to you. I'll make your day."

"Dump the phone and get another one. I'll put in a voucher for you."

"Bye, sweetheart. Sunshine out." The phone went dead.

Halloran sank back in his chair. *Jesus Christ, six mil. Nothing this big for years.* He smiled and thought quietly to himself.

Chapter 8

The storm blew itself out quickly and the morning began sparkling and fresh. Angie was up first, waking Hughes when she started the coffee grinder. He could see her through the open bedroom door, puttering nude in the kitchen, and he lay motionless admiring her taut legs and breasts. He congratulated himself again. She was peering into the refrigerator when he came up behind and hugged her with both arms. She jumped and giggled. "Back off, bad boy, I'm working a double today. No time for play."

Hughes feigned sadness then grinned at her. "Don't forget about tomorrow," he said.

"What's tomorrow? It's Saturday."

"Remember the cookout down at Bill Halloran's"

"Oh, Jesus. It's in the burbs. Do we have to? It'll be painful." Angie said as she placed milk and bread on the counter and walked into the bedroom to throw on a short silk robe.

"This sounds familiar. Come on, Angie. You know how important it is for me to have a contact in the Bureau. Let's make the most of it."

"Can't we do dinner here in the city with them? We

could go to the outdoor café at Abe & Louie's and you can impress him."

"I committed. I think it may be just the four of us. Got to do it." Hughes pleaded.

"Christ. Ok. What time and what do I wear?"

"It's in the afternoon. We should get there about one o'clock. Be back here by the evening. Wear that blue summer dress with the scoop neck. That'll get his attention."

"Yeah, and his wife's as well. What's her name?"

"It's Laura. I think you'll get along fine."

"What I don't do for you. You owe me big time. Now help me tidy up. I've got to get myself together and ready for the lunch crowd of Friday animals."

Hughes spent the rest of the morning doing paperwork and managed to get several invoices ready to mail. He felt good about getting caught up. He then wandered over to LA Sports, and spent the next three hours working out and ogling the talent there. It turned into a lazy summer day and he relished it. They were few and far between lately. Feeling hungry, he headed to the bar where Angie was working. He ordered food and watched her finish up the long day, annoying her by making faces from time to time.

He waited for her to tip out and they walked together under a starry indigo sky back to Joy Street. They were slow and calm with each other during the night, letting the sweetness develop. The end came not as an explosion, but with the deliberateness of an opening flower.

*　*　*

Route 3 to the South Shore was busy on a summer Saturday. Hughes had the top down on the Miata. He was wearing a ball cap with a "B" on it; Angie a cap with "NY" on the front, and they got stares as they passed several large SUV's laden with vacation gear heading for the Cape.

The Halloran house was a neat light blue ranch on a street of immaculate ranches and colonials. Lawn care seemed to be a high priority in the area. The only cars in the driveway were Bill's SUV, and a cream colored Prius, probably Laura's, when Hughes wedged his tiny sports car in. They knocked on the front door with no response, so Hughes tried the door, found it unlocked and called in. A voice from the back called to them to come in and they stepped gingerly into a family room with a vaulted ceiling. Through the back window, Hughes saw smoke rising from a large silver grill and he glimpsed the svelte and attractive Laura, wearing a pink apron over jeans and a t-shirt, setting an oval table.

"Hey," Bill Halloran yelled out, coming around the corner with a tall glass in his hand. "How about a Tanqueray and tonic? I've got a pitcher full." He was grinning and his face was flushed.

"Sounds good," Hughes replied, and looked at Angie, who nodded uncertainly.

Drinks were served and streaks were grilled. Laura came out of the kitchen with a crisp tomato and cucumber salad and a stack of foil wrapped baked potatoes. She pulled off her apron when she sat down, and it was obvious she was not wearing a bra. Hughes asked for another cocktail.

The picnic style lunch, served in the freshly mowed backyard surrounded by colorful impatients, was delicious. Angie changed drinks and sipped white wine, as did Laura, while Hughes had trouble keeping up with Halloran's drinking. The tone was relaxed and friendly, with

Halloran spinning a couple of very off-color jokes, which Hughes appreciated more than the women did.

After they ate, Halloran's son Bobby came out to the yard. Only sixteen, he had multiple piercings in his ears and wore his hair spiked. His jeans rode low, exposing the elastic strip of his Hanes underwear. He ignored Bill and went to Laura. "I need eighty dollars right away," he demanded.

Laura looked at him, confused by the interruption, and replied, "What? What for?"

"I owe a guy and I need it right away. Doesn't concern you," he replied.

Bill looked up with a drink in his hand and said, "What the hell is the matter with you? Don't you have any manners barging in like this?"

"Just give me the fucking eighty and I'll get out of here." Everyone in the yard was quiet, watching.

Bill glared at him for a moment, then reached into his pocket, peeled off four twenties and handed them to Bobby. "Here, now get the hell out of here. We'll talk later."

Bobby took the money and stuffed it into the back pocket of his jeans. He walked back into the house without another word. Bill stared after him. He then turned back and muttered, "Happy family life." The tension broke.

An hour later, Halloran was showing the effects of his multiple gin and tonics. Surprisingly, Angie and Laura seemed to be getting along nicely, although Hughes was sure Laura gave him a couple of lascivious looks during the meal.

"Danny, come on inside. I want to show you the new sig the Bureau gave me." Bill said.

Hughes shrugged, stood up unsteadily and followed Bill through the back door. Halloran led him into the bedroom, which was oddly decorated with colonial furniture, lace curtains and a white shag rug. He reached into the closet and removed a square side arm in a tan hip holster. He pulled the gun out, checked the magazine and handed it to Hughes.

"Nice balance," Hughes said.

"Yeah," said Halloran, smiling. Then he said, "Danny, I've got an idea that could be a life altering event." He suddenly seemed calm and sober. "I've got a CI in Miami who tells me about a drug deal going down. We're talking about maybe six mil in cash being carried up north by the bad guys."

"Sounds like a nice bust for you guys."

"I was thinking of something a little different. What if the six mil ends up in our hands? All cash. All untraceable."

Hughes thought for a moment. "You talking about ripping off the mule?"

"Who are they going to call? The cops? Especially if they think it's some of their guys. Easy to do."

"I think they would be seriously pissed off. I don't think I need a bunch of pissed off drug dealers looking for me."

"No one would ever know. This is very closed circuit info. Nobody knows about this, not even my office."

Hughes was silent for a minute. "Let me think about it. I think you're fuckin nuts."

"Don't think too much. I think this is going down in the next couple of weeks. We can plan it out and walk away with no more problems. Let's have a drink tomorrow and talk some more."

"I don't know," Hughes said hesitantly. "Ok, we'll talk more about it tomorrow. Let's go have another cocktail."

Chapter 9

The sun was a shimmering pumpkin dropping in the sky when Hughes and Angie finally left. He up-shifted clumsily as they headed onto the northbound ramp of Route 3 and back to the city. A heavy weariness was with them in the small car as Hughes brought it up to a steady speed in the right lane.

"Wasn't that just special?" Angie whispered.

Hughes was silent. After a couple of minutes, he said, "What do you think of that all-American lifestyle?"

"If that is what I have to look forward to, kill me now." She paused. "How about that kid?"

"I hear the daughter is worse."

"God, how old is she?"

"Fourteen."

"Jesus. And that Laura has the hots for you," Angie said.

Hughes looked over at her. Cut it out, Angie. You're not getting a jealousy streak, are you?"

Angie sighed. "Don't tell me you didn't notice. Christ, her nipples got hard every time she stood within five feet of you."

Hughes laughed.

Traffic came to a crawl as the highway filled with sun-burned beachgoers heading home. The Miata was dwarfed by SUVs crammed inside and out with gear. Hughes found some soft jazz on the radio and they sat listening without a word in the stop and go jam.

After a while, Hughes said, "Is that where we are headed?"

"Right now, we'd be lucky to be able to afford that. That is, if we stay together. Who knows?"

"With enough money, we could break away from all of that."

"Yeah, with enough money people can do anything, even make themselves miserable. I've got to get a lot more tips before I even think about moving to the burbs." They were both silent for several moments.

The traffic slowly began to break free and Hughes brought the car back to a reasonable speed, turning onto the expressway and toward the soft focus of city lights. They passed the Dorchester Yacht Club, where boats sat idle on glassy water, the day's adventures over. As they came up Beacon Hill, they saw a few strollers moving slowly in the heavy summer heat. Hughes and Angie were too emotionally tired to talk more.

Chapter 10

The low ranch sat unimposing among the garish mansions in Sunny Isles on the Intercoastal up from Miami Beach. Ciracero herded his Bentley behind a black Lincoln Navigator and a large, low and wide object covered by a tan car cover. Each time he came to this place he felt a dim anxiety and today was no exception.

He rang the bell and was met by a copper skinned giant in a baggy Tommy Bahama shirt. Ciracero worked on a sincere smile, "Is he in?"

The giant nodded and stepped aside. The sunken living room looked out to a boat dock, where a white inboard runabout sat suspended in the glare of the harsh Florida sun. In front of an enormous television sat three men watching a golf match. Each held a sweating rocks glass. All three were engrossed in the TV, and at once let out a collective groan.

"Dumb shit," Sal Tessio yelled at the television, then looked over to where Ciracero stood just outside the sunken living room. "You are really fuckin ugly," he said to him.

"Hi, Sal. How ya doin?" Ciracero spoke louder than he intended.

"I'm doin. What have you got for me?" Sal heaved himself off the couch. His paunch did not disguise the thick muscles. He was dark, but less tan than the other two men, who were still engrossed in the golf game. He wore off-white linen pants, cinched at the waist and a dark blue Hawaiian shirt. On his feet were, Mephisto sandals and white socks.

"They are ready to do business." Ciracero said confidently. "They want to know the level of business you are thinking."

"I'm thinking I can buy out the whole fucking country. I got Constantine in Boston going in with me. We're talking three to four mil each. Can they meet that level of business?'

"I think so. They act like they can do anything. Should I set it up?"

Sal stared at him with snake eyes. "Yeah, asshole, set it up. You know Paul's boat at Pier 66?"

"Sal, how does my cut look?" Ciracero said uncertainly.

Sal said nothing, and turned back to look at the television for a minute. "Dumb fuck," he said to it. Then, over his shoulder, "Yeah, asshole, just don't fuck it up." Still looking at the set, he plopped back onto the couch. The other two men sipped at their drinks, and one glanced over at Ciracero.

Ciracero walked out stronger than he walked in. He got into his car, took a deep breath and headed slowly toward the causeway. After five minutes on the road, he called Hornez.

"Hey amigo," Ciracero said into the phone with a smile.

"What's up? You sound like a day at the beach."

"Hey friend, you still got those Cuban broads on a string? I need to party."

"Not only those two, they have a friend who joins in. But, together they're not cheap."

"Tell them I want all night. All three. They get a good tip if I'm happy. You can join in too, my treat."

"You stick up a liquor store or something?"

"It's going down, buddy boy, and I get a piece of the action. Maybe as much as six mil. That will be some fucking finder's fee."

"I'm in the mood for a party, especially on your nickel. Why don't I get a suite at the Fontainebleau, high up with a view? I'll get the booze and the ladies. You get your wallet. I can be there by six. Meet me at the lobby bar."

Three hours later, Ciracero rushed into the soaring lobby of the Fontainebleau and found Hornez sitting at the large square bar reading *Racing News*.

"Horseman," he called out, as he walked up to Hornez, and signaled the bartender at the same time. "I hope you are good to your word as I am fuckin' ready to party. Did you get three?"

Hornez smiled. "I sent the girls up to fill up the ice buckets and enjoy the view. We will be enjoying the view all night, if you know what I mean."

Downing his drink fast, Ciracero was anxious to go upstairs to the women. The suite had a sweeping view of the enormous pool, backed by the aquamarine Atlantic. The three women were stunning and Hornez introduced them as he walked into the suite. "We have here for our dining pleasure Jan, Rosie and Maria. Let's all have a drink and get acquainted."

Jan smiled broadly and started filling glasses with ice. She was wearing a silk summer pullover dress, and when she bent over to scoop the ice, her left breast, darkly tanned and pink tipped, slipped out. When she straightened, she made no effort to place it back inside her thin dress.

Chapter 11

The late morning was already scalding and the relentless sun made the pavements as soft as pizza dough. Ciracero cruised the Bentley slowly into the parking lot of Pier 66. The great car was silent except for the tires, which sizzled on the hot blacktop. The lot was strewn with pricey cars, mostly silver or black in color, parked like scattered pieces of of a broken expensive necklacein random fashion. He noted no foot traffic as he maneuvered the Bentley into an open space.

He exited and made his way past the main building to the slips, walking down the ramp and past blindingly white boats sitting haughtily in the serene harbor. At the end of the ramp he saw a fifty something foot Hatteras with some activity on its stern.

Ciracero paused at the gangplank leading up to make sure. A dark skinned man, shirtless with a sculpted chest, peered over and waved him up. As Ciracero stepped on board, he was momentarily unnerved at the sight of two stunning women lying indifferently topless on deck, each wearing hudge sunglasses and holding sweating cocktail glasses. Just inside the cabin, through the closed slider, he saw four men sitting around a teak table. The man who had gestured to Ciracero sat down next to the women, ignoring them and looked toward the pier.

Unsure what to do, Ciracero stood awkwardly outside until one of the men at the table waved him in. He pulled the slider open and was hit with icy cold air. The four men offered no greeting, until the one closest to him, a swarthy man with black hair slicked straight back and large diamonds in both ears, told him to sit on a drop-down shelf. Three of the men were thickly muscular and appeared to be in their thirties. The fourth, sitting furthest away was an older man with long, thick, white hair that highlighted his dark tan and deep brown eyes. He regarded Ciracero with disdain. Tension and fear filled the chilly cabin.

One of the younger men, heavyset with a large belly, said, "So, you bring us news from your people?" He spoke with a lisp and in a surprisingly high tone.

Ciracero gave a weak smile to the group and tried to compose himself. "I have good news from my people. They wish to make a substantial contribution."

The older man sat silent, exuding menace. The man to his left, wearing an oversized Hawaiian shirt, glanced around the small table at his companions and then back to Ciracero. His eyes were widely spread and sat reptilian blank over a nose that looked to have been broken repeatedly. He said in a whisper, "You are the representative?"

"I am the initial contact. My people want you to know they are ready with six to eight," Ciracero replied.

The four men looked at each other without comment or expression.

"How can they do this?" he asked.

Ciracero took a deep breath. "Three groups. Here and New York and Boston. They control the Northeast."

After minutes of dead silence, the man on the left

called out to the man on the stern, "Pauly, anything going on?"

"No one around," was the reply.

"Step outside. Stay with the putas," the first man said coldly and Ciracero stepped out into the solid heat as he was told. The sliding door to the cabin slid shut with a metallic click, and the heat poured over him like a blast furnace. He nodded to the shirtless man, who ignored him and continued to watch the pier. The two women glanced at him and giggled. Ciracero sat across the stern from the other occupants and sweated profusely, soaking his flowered shirt through in seconds. He could see the men in conversation inside the cabin.

Finally, the first man signaled him to come back in. Again, the cold air hit him like a fist and for a second, Ciracero felt dangerously dizzy. The older man spoke for the first time.

"Where is it coming from?" He had a deep baritone voice and a commanding tone.

"Here and New York and Boston," Ciracero said. "Equal partners." Ciracero thought he saw pink in the man's eyes.

"You guarantee this?" he asked. "How?"

"They request the product is brought to New York. The Boston side will be there and you do one deal, at one time. You pick the place and the time. These are stand up guys."

The man grunted. "Go outside."

It seemed even hotter as he stepped through the slider again. One of the women appeared to be asleep, the other rocking to music plugged into her ears from an iPod. He waited.

His lips started to parch and he felt soaked at his crotch

under the white linen pants. A few agonizing minutes later, big belly came out. He was thick through the shoulders and Ciracero noticed for the first time a deep scar across his neck. He held out a small piece of paper.

"Buy a phone and call this number and leave the number of the phone you bought. After we call, destroy your phone. Any fuck-ups, it's not good for you."

Ciracero walked out past the two women and the lookout, who paid no attention to him. He made his way unsteadily onto the dock and back toward the tower of the hotel. His head was spinning furiously in the aftermath of the meeting and the cold finger of fear remained. As he walked through the stifling parking lot to the Bentley, he smiled weakly and pulled out his phone. "Horseman, I told you I could pull this off."

Hornez, who was driving across the Causeway with the top down on his Mustang, could barely hear over the traffic. "What happened?"

"I got the deal going. I'm heading across the Intercoastal to talk to the boys and get it down solid. I think I just made some serious bucks in finder's fees. I'm the man."

Chapter 12

Shortly after dusk, the house on Sunny Isles lit up like a carnival ride. Exterior lights shown upwards on the palm trees and the security lights on the dock sparkled on the water of the Intercoastal. A deep glow emerged from the thick windows of the house allowed a thin glow to emerge,, but the denseness of the glass prevented any inward views. A skinny man in a black t-shirt and slacks sat in a chaise, smoking a coal colored cigar. Despite the excessive lighting, he was the only sign of outside activity.

Inside, four men sat on the white leather furniture. Ciracero knocked and was let in. He nodded to the men and nervously stood next to a large couch.

Sal Tessio took a sip from a crystal glass and said to Ciracero, "You think they are serious?" It sounded more like a statement than a question.

Ciracero nodded. "Boss, I'm telling you, this deal will work. They are just as worried you can't do the cash as you are about their quantity."

"We put it together with enough security, we got no worries," Tessio said to the other men.

Johnnie Lugar, slumped deep into the upholstery of a chair too big for him, said, "We do two, Boston does two, New York another two, we pick up twelve in product, maybe more if we split right. Question is, can we move it?"

Muciello, in from New York, his white socks stark against black alligator wing tip shoes, said quietly, "I got guys in Harlem, Brighton Beach and a yuppie asshole in the city. We can move ours. Question is, can Boston move theirs?"

Tessio responded back, "Their problem. Constantine said he's in if we let him. If he has to snort it himself, he'll find a way to move the shit."

Still standing nervously, Ciracero tried to light a cigarette but had trouble with his Dunhill lighter. Finally getting it going, he inhaled deeply and exhaled a thick cloud of smoke. After a minute, Tessio said to him, "Gimme the fuckin' phone."

Ciracero handed over the small black unit he bought. "Here's the number," he said. He pulled out a twenty-dollar bill and read off the numbers he had written on it.

Tessio punched in the numbers and waited. Then, "It's me. We are OK here. We'll make arrangements as to date, time and place and asshole will visit you again."

He was silent as he listened. "OK, we are all a go. We need two weeks. I'm smashing this phone and tossing the pieces in the canal." He hit the disconnect button and dropped the phone on the marble floor. He reached into a drawer in the side table, pulled out a heavy handgun and hit the phone twice with the butt of it. It cracked into four pieces. He looked up at Ciracero, "Pick up this shit and throw it in the canal at different places. You understand?

Ciracero nodded.

Tessio, turning away, said in a whisper, " Come here in two days at six o'clock. You can go back and visit them again then." The other three men sipped their drinks and smiled.

Ciracero walked outside grinning broadly. The man in the black t-shirt stood up and stared. Ciracero put up his hands and the man sat down again as he walked past him to his Bentley. He was heading down Collins with the windows down when he called again, talking loudly into his hands-free. "Horseman, I told you. It's a go. Six, maybe eight big ones. Meet me at the Bleau and order a bottle of Patron."

Hornez, sitting in a Cuban restaurant eating a pork dinner with the owner of a car dealership, said, "Jesus. You shittin me? What's your take?"

A soft evening wind blew through the car window. Ciracero said, "I'm looking at a half percent. Maybe three hundred K. I can take it in cash or product. I'll take the cash, thank you."

"I'm happy for you. When's this going to happen?"

"I figure in about two weeks. I'll know for sure in two days when they give me the details to deliver. I think I'll go down to St. Barts and fuck around for a week. In the meantime, meet me for a drink. I'm in a really good mood."

"Sure, same place in an hour," said Hornez, and snapped his phone shut. He turned to his dinner companion and said, "I got to go out to make a call. Be right back." He was already standing up and trying to remember the number.

Halloran was sitting comfortably in a side chair in the front lounge section of Mistral, nursing his second Macallan, when one of his phones buzzed. He patted his jacket and pants pockets until he found the buzzing one. Only one person had that number. He answered, "Yes?"

Hornez said, "It's me"

"Yes," he said quietly.

"It's going down. A big one," Hornez said, standing outside next to a palm tree.

"How big and when?" Halloran asked.

"Maybe about six, could be more. Maybe in about two weeks," Hornez replied.

Halloran was silent. Then, "I'll need all the details. Throw that phone away and call me when you know."

"You got it." Hornez clicked off. Halloran took a large swig of his scotch and replayed the conversation in his head.

Five minutes later he grinned when he saw Hughes being greeted by the striking hostess with the short black dress cut low across the top. She pointed to Halloran, who stuck up his arm to wave Hughes over. Halloran continued to grin at Hughes as he settled into a chair.

"What's happening, Bill?" Hughes asked as a cocktail waitress glided over to him. He looked up at her and signaled he'd have the same as Halloran. She smiled, looked at Halloran's glass and glided away.

The lounge was decorated in contrasting shades of Armani gray. Filtered light glowed through the enormous curtained front windows. The place was filled with the usual crowd of arrogant stock traders, trophy wives and mistresses. The bar was buzzing. Two blondes in short shift dresses were seated on stools at one corner, drawing lots of attention.

Halloran grinned at Hughes. "You are a lucky guy to know me," he said.

Hughes did not reply, but waited for the next line.

Halloran took a deep sip of his cocktail, leaned over to Hughes and whispered, "It's going down. How would you like to split about six mil, maybe more, tax free, hassle free?"

Hughes felt a nervous pit in his stomach. He waited, wanting and not wanting to hear more.

"My CI gave it to me tonight. About six mil, maybe more, coming up in a couple of weeks. I should know all the details. All we have to do is just take it away."

Hughes thought for a minute then asked, "How the hell can we get away with this?"

Halloran smiled. "Shit, man. Who they gonna call? It's dirty money from dirty maggots doing dirty business. We would be doing the world a favor."

"I don't know. I've got to think about it," Hughes said.

"Nothing to think about. I'll set it up. All you've got to do is work with me. We split fifty-fifty." Halloran signaled to the waitress for another round.

Hughes ate a margherita pizza while Halloran drank another scotch and sent over two cosmopolitans to the blondes at the bar. They accepted with cold smiles, lifting their glasses in a toast, then turning away.

"Cunts," Halloran muttered as Hughes got up to leave.

"Got to go. Big day tomorrow. Let's talk more." Hughes threw down two twenties.

"OK, buddy boy," Halloran said. "Think about it. If we do this, we can have blondes like those crawling on their knees after us. I'll call you tomorrow and we can plan this out."

"Talk to you tomorrow," Hughes said as he walked out without a glance to the hostess, who was trying to thank him.

Chapter 13

He headed home, walking across the Boston Common under a soft summer glow, to Beacon Hill and his apartment. The foyer light was out, giving the entrance a foreboding feel. Climbing the wooden stairs, he unlocked his door and walked in without turning on the lights. He maneuvered around using just the street light that filtered in. He found an Amstel Light beer in the refrigerator and plopped down into his worn chair to think. He rolled over Halloran's idea, and couldn't think of many risks. The reward was certainly appealing. He sat there in the dusky dark until he heard the front door buzzer. Angie's familiar steps were approaching and she let herself in with her key.

"Jesus," she said. "Turn on some lights."

"No problem," Hughes said, getting up and heading back to the kitchen to search for another beer.

Angie knew where he was going and called out, "Get one for me, too."

He found one more in the back of the refrigerator and split it into two glasses, bringing them back into the living area where Angie had sat down on the couch. He placed one next to her on the end table. She reached for it and placed the cold glass against her forehead. Her white blouse looked lived in and her black skirt had hiked up to mid-thigh. Even in the dim light, Hughes could see the weariness that hung on her like a woolen cape.

"Jesus, sometimes I hate that place." Taking a sip, she asked, "So I hope your day was better than mine. The customers in my joint are a bunch of mindless yahoos. Most of the guys in there wear their ball caps on backwards, looking like retards. Twice I got my ass patted as I tried to serve tables."

Hughes was silent for a minute. Then he said, "Angie, where the fuck are we going?"

Angie finished her beer in a gulp and said, "I know where I'm going. I'm getting out of that dump of a bar."

"No, I mean long term. Are we going to be shuffling along like this ten years from now?"

Angie looked at him. "Are you talking about us, or life in general?"

"I don't know. Maybe both."

She got up, walked to the refrigerator and rummaged around inside. She came back with a bottle of water and uncapped it before answering. "I know one thing, Danny. There is more to life than smiling at morons at a bar and shacking up with you. My clock is ticking away and sooner or later I have to figure out something else."

Hughes talked low. "Angie, what if I had a chance to do a real score. One that would let us do whatever we wanted?"

"I take it you are not talking the lottery and not talking legally," she said.

"Maybe something that is low risk and high reward. Something that only comes around once. If I took a chance, would you stick around?"

She got up, walked to the window and looked out at

Joy Street. It was deserted with the soft focus light of in the hot summer evening. She could see some dog walkers in the Common and a sports car, top down, rocketing down Beacon Street.

She said, "Danny, don't do anything stupid. Most people do fine working away and moving forward. I don't need anything that is not earned or can hurt you or me."

"Don't worry, Angie. I won't do anything stupid. He stood and walked over to her. He put his arm around her gently, feeling the dampness of her sweat. He cupped her full breast through her blouse. Trying to change the mood, he said, "The beer is gone so get out of those waitress clothes and let me give you a massage."

She looked up into his eyes with apprehension. That night, for the first time with him, Angie faked her orgasm.

Chapter 14

Tessio sat his considerable bulk on a wicker stool at the bar near the far end of the infinity pool behind the Delano. Ciracero stood nervously next to him. They were watching the scene at the pool where several attractive people lounged and floated. Occasionally one or two of the women would laugh or squeal. Tessio had his catcher's mitt hand wrapped around a rocks glass, and Ciracero swilled down his third Corona.

"See that cabana over there?" Tessio gestured toward a three-sided cabana on the other side of the room. "Last time I was here, some babe gave a guy a blowjob in there. No one paid any attention." He laughed to himself. Then he turned toward Ciracero with a complete shift in mood and said darkly, "So where are these guys? Is it set up or what?"

Ciracero chain-smoked and said, "Hey, they'll be here. This is a win-win for everyone. They sat in silence. After a while three men came through the rear door of the hotel and walked with purpose across the lawn toward them. Two wore off-white linen and the third wore a garish shirt not tucked in.

Ciracero said, "Here we go."

The men came up to the bar and looked around. Tessio gestured to a table secluded in the corner and said, "We can talk there." Without a word, the group moved to the table and sat down. The air seemed to thicken.

Ciracero started. "Guys, this is Sal Tessio. He will do the deal with you."

They nodded, still silent. Tessio said, "OK, we are ready. We have New York and Boston with us. We will buy 200 keys, delivered to New York." He puffed up slightly and looked back and forth to the three Columbians. Ciracero recognized two of them from the boat. The third, a wiry, deeply tanned man somewhere between forty and sixty years old, was new. His eyes were as dead as marbles. After a moment he spoke. "We've checked you out and feel you are men of your word. We can deliver the product. Forty a key. "Forty?" Tessio coughed. "We are buying quantity. We will pay thirty."

The other two men looked at the older man. He stared unblinking at Tessio. Tension rose. Noise from the pool seemed to disappear. After a minute, he said,

"Thirty-five. Please do not waste our time. You can test it. However, we need two million in advance." He stared directly and steadily at Tessio.

Tessio stared back. He waited then said, "We have a special vehicle arranged for transport to New York. We have it lined up to make the deal work. You can trust us. I will meet your price, but why do you need the advance?"

"This is how we do business. You will take the product to New York and sell it for whatever you want. You will bring back four more to us immediately. That is trust." One of the other men nodded. The older man took out a cigar from his shirt pocket and lit it slowly and deliberately. He waited. Then he said to one of the other men,

"Where are your manners? Give our new friend a cigar so he can smoke with me." Immediately, another long cigar was produced and handed to Tessio. The Columbian leaned over with a gold lighter and lit the cigar for him.

After both were smoldering, Tessio said, "OK, let us know where we can get the product. We will have the down payment when we test it. If all is well, it will move to New York, payments will be made and the balance will be back here within a week." Smoke curled around the table like thinning fog. After a minute, a cell phone was handed to Ciracero. The older man said, "We will call this number in a day. You answer by saying, 'Yo, yo.' You will be given an address. Once you hear that, you destroy the phone. If we do not see anyone in twenty-four hours, we cancel. Understood?"

Tessio smiled for the first time. A loud female squeal came from the pool. No one paid any notice. Putting down the cigar, Tessio stuck out his catcher's mitt of a fist and shook hands all around. The three Columbians stood, nodded slightly and moved away past the pool. Tessio and Ciracero watched them leave through the rear doors.

Ciracero grinned. "We got a deal. Don't forget me."

Tessio looked at him like he was something stuck to his shoe. "We never renege. You will get what's coming to you."

Ciracero looked at him. "Take care of me.. I helped with a monster deal.

What is it worth in New York?" Ciracero asked.

Tessio glared back. "What we sell it for is our business. You what you get,, which will be worth more than you are. Now get out of here and come to me as soon as you get the call."

Ciracero stood and sighed, knowing there was no

negotiation. "Great doing business," he said uncertainly. Walking off, he smiled at a young woman in a black thong sitting at the edge of the pool. He walked through the lobby with its shimmering diaphanous drapes and called for the Bentley from the valet. He put the top down on the car, took out his own cigar and lit it before driving off. As he pulled onto Ocean Drive, he speed-dialed Hornez.

"Amigo, booze and broads are on me. I just scored a great deal."

Hornez sat up in the chaise and looked around. The pool behind his condo was deserted. "What's the deal?"

Two hundred keys are coming our way and heading north. Looks like I'm in for a piece of six mil. Eat your fucking heart out."

"You're shitting me. When's this happening?"

"Soon, amigo. In the meantime, meet me at the Bleau and kiss my ring."

"OK. When?"

"Now, I'm on my way. I'll be at the bar, looking rich."

"See you there." Hornez looked around and fished the extra phone from his bag. He dialed Boston and settled back.

Chapter 15

Two days later, the little phone rang. Dozing on the couch during a Yankees game, Ciracero at first couldn't figure out where the sound was coming from. Then like a bolt, it hit him and he grabbed for it off the coffee table. "Hello, I mean yo, yo." He stumbled.

An accented voice said, "2084 Southwest 184th. South Miami Heights. Tomorrow at 6. Bring only two guys." The call clicked off. Ciracero sat for a minute collecting his thoughts. "It's going down," he said to himself. He pocketed the phone and picked up another one to call Tessio.

The following afternoon was steaming, with dark gray downspouts visible to the north. Ciracero was driving a four door Ford F-150 pickup with a cap on the back. Tessio sat in the passenger seat. The windows were rolled up and the air conditioner was on high, blasting ice cold air into their faces. Traffic bumped along slowly and Tessio said, "The backup is already there in a white van. Don't look at it."

The building was a low, wooden structure, white paint peeling from the rotting wood. Ciracero pulled up in front of the dented, rusty overhead door and waited. After a minute, the door slowly slid upwards. Inside stood four men, two of which Ciracero recognized from the talks; two others were very dark skinned hulking figures. Each was holding a short, mean automatic weapon loosely in their hands. The pickup came to a stop ten feet inside. Light filtered in from cracked and broken skylights, the sun illuminated floating dust as it poured through the dirty windows. Ciracero and Tessio sat in the truck, waiting. After a minute, the obvious leader, gestured for them to approach. They emerged slowly from the cab and took three or four steps in his direction. Both Tessio and Ciracero held their hands up.

The handsome man from the meeting at the Delano took a step forward and said, "Where is our advance?"

Tessio replied, "Where is our product?"

The Columbian gestured him forward. He said to Ciracero, "You stay there." Ciracero did.

Tessio was led to a corner of the warehouse. There sat a U-Haul box trailer. The rear door was pulled open to reveal stacks of tightly wrapped cellophane packages, each about six inches by four inches. Tesso took out a switchblade knife, popped it open and stuck it in one of the packages. He wet his finger and stuck it in the slit. He then placed his finger, with white powder on the tip, in his mouth. After a minute, he nodded.

"So where is our money?" The leader of the men asked.

Tessio looked hard at him. "Outside there is a white van with tinted windows. Inside the van are three of my men. They are not nice men but they can be nice today. Load up the product into our truck. When that's done, I make a phone call to the van. I have a special way of talking to them so they know it's me and that I'm okay. They will then back the van up to the door. You will open the door and they will transfer the money to you. You can keep the door half closed so we can't drive our truck out until you are satisfied. OK?"

The man stood silent for a minute. Then he said to the armed men, "Start loading it up."

Tessio then called out to Ciracero. "Open it up."

Ciracero reached into the cab, and took out a long metal bar with a hook on the end. He walked around to the back of the truck and stuck the bar into a small slot in the side. The false bottom in the bed of the truck popped up exposing the actual bed of the truck. The Columbian smiled and nodded to his men who started placing the small packages side by side from the trailer to the truck. He said to the men, "We only have less than four inches of clearance so lay them in a single row. Within minutes, one hundred and seventy of the small packages were neatly laid in the truck bed.

"Make your call," he said to Tessio. Tessio pulled out a small cell phone, touched the button for the programmed number and spoke softly into the phone. Outside, the van could be faintly heard pulling up to the overhead door. The Columbian then opened it halfway to reveal the rear of the van, its rear doors open and three men with shotguns peering out. Tessio bent over, walked out of the half opened overhead door and stood next to the van. He said to the men in the van, "Place one satchel on the ground in front of the door." Then to the Columbian, "Count it. I'll get into my truck with my driver and drive out as they put the other satchel down. Don't bother to shake hands."

While the men with the Uzis watched, the leader knelt down and quickly determined that one million dollars was there. He stood up and turned to Tessio. "Place the rest of the money on the ground. Once I look inside, and see that it is all there, I will open the door all the way and your friend can drive out. We will consider our business done. Men of their word live longer than cheaters. You understand?" Tessio nodded and climbed into the pickup. The other satchel was tossed out of the van, and fifteen minutes later, while Tessio and Ciracero stood and watched, the money in the second satchel was counted. Receiving a nod, they got in the pickup, started it and drove out. The van followed. About two blocked away, Ciracero wiped his hand across his face and grinned over at Tessio. "Good job, boss. We're on our way." Tessio looked back at Ciracero with distaste and said nothing.

They parked the truck inside a garage next to a house that was for sale on Byron Avenue in Surfside. Tessio owned the property. He had equipped the cinder block garage with special alarms and locks six months ago. But he was still uneasy about keeping the stash there, and made calls to arrange moving it north. Two days later, he sent Ciracero and a goon they called Toady, for obvious reasons, to the garage. He was waiting when they arrived.

"You guys will drive this truck to an address I will give you in two days. I expect you to be very close to where I will be sending you, by then." Tessio said.

"Right, boss." Ciracero looked nervously at Toady, who was wearing a black tee shirt, stretched taunt over his chest and biceps and was picking his teeth with a plastic toothpick.

Twelve hours later, Ciracero and Toady loaded up four thermos of coffee and a bag of white bread sandwiches. Toady was wearing a Gold's Gym t-shirt and black jeans and was carrying a gym bag. Ciracero wore his usual Hawaiian shirt until Tessio told him to take it off and made him put on a blue polo. They sat and waited while Tessio left to make a series of calls. He was back in an hour.

"You move out on Monday. Go get laid or get some sleep or something and be back here early Monday morning."

Ciracero thought the getting laid idea was a good one and called Horseman to set it up again.

Chapter 16

Hughes woke to a pounding in his head. "Jesus," he thought to himself, "checked three bars, had two drinks in each, and then had a late drink with Angie when she finished her shift. Made four hundred dollars. Wonder how much a new liver will cost?" He slowly realized the pounding was coming from his door, a consistent and unrelenting knocking. He pulled himself out of bed, padded to the door and looked through the peephole. Standing outside, his face distorted by the fish eye effect, was Halloran. Hughes opened the door, turned without a word and headed toward the kitchen and his coffee pot. "What do you want?" he said over his shoulder, as he poured water into the machine.

"We have to talk. Jesus, put some pants on," Halloran said. Hughes gave him a look as he returned to the bedroom, picked up his pants off the floor and pulled them on.

"I say again," Hughes muttered, returning to the kitchen, "What the fuck do you want?"

"Get some coffee in you so you can think straight and then sit down. I've got the offer of a lifetime, buddy boy." Hughes sat at the pine table, ran a hand through his hair and looked at Halloran. Halloran smiled back. After a minute, the coffee was done. Hughes poured a cup, sat back down and took a sip. "What?"

Halloran started in right away. "I got word from my CI in Miami. The scumbags there did a six mil deal with the Columbians and are driving it to New York to sell at profit. Guess who is going to relieve them of that profit?"

Hughes took another sip of coffee before replying. "How do you propose to do that? And, are you fucking nuts?"

Halloran chuckled. "Look, I'm the only one who knows this. According to my snitch, only two guys are coming up from Miami to do this deal. They are supposed to sell the coke, put four or six mil or whatever in their truck and drive it back south. We can certainly handle two guys. I will even make it look like New York did a double cross and ripped off the Miami boys. While they are wasting each other, we will be sitting pretty on a stack of happiness."

"How do we know where these guys are?" Hughes asked, trying to focus.

"This is the sweet part. According to my guy, this deal is so big it's being split between the New York, Miami and Boston boys. The Boston connection is Constantine and his crew. I know those assholes inside and out. All we have to do is tail whoever leaves from here to the city, wait until the full deal goes down and politely remove the money from the couriers before they head back. Sweet, and no one will know who the masked men are. And, like I said, who are they going to call?"

"You know, Bill, something always goes wrong. Don't you ever go to the movies?" Hughes's headache was fading away like morning fog, and lucidity was starting to kick in.

Halloran got up from the table and helped himself to a

cup of coffee. Then he went to the window and stared out at the trees hanging low in the August heat. After a few minutes of silence, he turned back, his voice low and serious. "Danny, this is simple and easy. I don't know about you, but I could use a couple mil. My kids are a nightmare and I practically have to force Laura to have sex with me. I'm up to my ass in bills with no end in sight. This could change everything. Look around at this dump. It's clear you could use a new start, too. This is a once in a lifetime opportunity."

Hughes was quiet, then let out a sigh. "OK, let's talk about it. But, if I think it's a fucking boondoggle, I'm out. How the hell are we going to tail whoever leaves from Boston?"

"Like I said, I'm so far up Constantine's asshole, I know every move he makes and who all his goons are. All we have to do is watch him at the right time and tail whoever leaves to New York. First chance, we stick a GPS on the car and monitor its movements. The New York and Boston people will have to join up to do the deal, so we let them do it together and watch who leaves. I even have a description of the truck they'll be driving up from Miami. It's got a false bottom in the bed, that's where they'll stash the coke. They'll have to stop sometime, at which point Batman and Robin will relieve them of their burden." Hughes shrugged and Halloran smiled. "Come on, put a shirt on and I'll buy you some breakfast. You look like shit."

The next morning a warm steady rain moved in, covering the streets in a pewter sheen. Hughes was on his laptop at the kitchen table with the window open, clicking through some almost past due reports when the phone rang.

It was Halloran. "O'Malley's, 11:30." Before Hughes could respond, the line went dead.

Hughes walked in at eleven forty-five, wet and dripping. Halloran was sitting in a rear booth and signaled by lifting his rocks glass. Hughes slid in opposite him. Halloran grinned and spoke in a hushed tone.

"I heard. The transport will take off next Monday. They plan to drive straight through to the city, taking about thirty-five hours or so. I figure our Boston dirt bags will start down on Tuesday sometime. You with me?"

"Jesus, Bill. You sure about this?" Hughes took off his Red Sox cap, shook the water off and placed it down next to him in the booth.

Halloran whispered, "We will do this and be back by Thursday, super rich. Piece of cake. The thing is, Danny, you can't say a word to anyone, especially Angie. And, we have to agree that once we grab the money, we lay low for a good while. We can't go around spending stupidly. We can't take off to parts unknown or do anything that may look suspicious. When we do the rip-off, snitches everywhere will be calling in as the boys on both sides start jumping through hoops."

"How can you make it look like a mob rip-off?" Hughes asked.

"Easy. I will tell my CI in Miami that we got information that a couple of the top soldiers in New York are shooting their mouths off and buying some new cars for cash. It'll get back to the Miami gang and back up to Boston in a day. They'll be shooting up each other's asses in no time. If we're cool, we stay away from the fray and sit tight."

"Two guys from Miami?" Hughes signaled to a waitress, who came over and took his order for a Bloody Mary. "Are they shooters?"

"Doesn't matter. They'll be dead tired and not expecting anything. We have the advantage. We relieve them of their burden, and tell them not to come back to New York again. We disable their vehicle, take away their phones and leave them sucking wind."

Hughes took a deep sip of his drink. "If it looks like a problem, we'll back off?"

"We are like the dark knights. If it's not going down as planned, we head home and forget the adventure. Put it in your book and publish it after you die."

Hughes was silent for a minute. "OK, I guess I'm in. Who takes care of what we need?" Hughes took another sip of his Bloody Mary. "Whose car do we use?"

Halloran settled back in the booth. He smiled at Hughes. "Danny, I'll take care of all logistics. I will rent a car under a different name. Change the plates to ones off a car that's been sitting in dead storage for a while that we confiscated from a New York doper. Even if someone gets a plate number, it'll go back to New York scumbags. I've got everything covered."

Hughes took another sip from his drink and stared out at the rain soaking the street. After a minute, he drained the glass and signaled for another.

Chapter 17

That weekend there was a hint of the end of summer as a cool breeze shifted in off the Atlantic. The city was filled with tourists milling around on street corners, holding up cartoon maps and pointing in different directions. Angie wanted to go to Newport, but Hughes had Red Sox tickets so they stayed home. It was an afternoon game, which was lost by the hometown heroes, so Hughes's anxiety was coated with depression. They walked to the Back Bay from Fenway Park, joining an unhappy and jostling crowd until they got to Abe & Louie's and found an outdoor table. The waiter appeared immediately and Hughes ordered a dry Ketel One martini. Angie ordered her usual un-oaked Chardonnay, which she sipped slowly. Hughes drained his martini and signaled for another before Angie had her second sip. She looked at him as he drank the second one half empty in a gulp.

"You know what they say about martinis, don't you?" she asked.

"Yeah, they're like breasts, one's not enough and three are too many."

"Are you going for the third?"

"So what if I do?" Hughes snapped back.

"It's only a baseball game. You know the Sox, they have to torture you." Angie took another tiny sip. It was hard to tell if any wine was gone from the glass.

"Screw the Sox." Hughes said. He settled back in his chair and watched the parade of swirling summer dresses and baggy Bermuda shorts moving along Boylston Street.

"What's the matter, Danny? You've been moody all weekend." Angie asked.

"Nothing's wrong," he said, draining the second martini and signaling for another. "I've got to go out of town for a couple of days. No big deal. I should be back by Wednesday or so."

She took another small sip. "Possible to tell me what it's about?" Angie asked quietly, sensing trouble.

"Nothing. Just business. But if I'm lucky, we should be in good shape."

Angie was silent. She stared out at the busy street and the crowds of mostly smiling people, then looked down at the snowy white tablecloth and shook her head.

Their lovemaking last night had been automatic and without energy. Hughes had been an indifferent lover. She wondered what was going on with him.

When they got back to Hughes's apartment Angie left early, telling him she had laundry and errands to do. Hughes sat by himself sipping leftover scotch and watching television without really paying attention. A dark anxiety hung over him like a funeral dirge.

Chapter 18

Three days later, Hughes got an urgent call from Halloran. "Grab your overnight bag and meet me on the corner of Beacon Street. We're on the move."

Hughes took his pre-packed bag from the closet, put on expensive Nike running shoes, worn jeans and a twill shirt. He swapped his Red Sox cap for a New York Yankees one and ran out to the street. Beacon Street was busy and the day looked normal, but Hughes did not feel normal. Doubt had settled in like a rash that would not go away.

Five minutes later, Halloran pulled up fast in a Ford Explorer, causing a young woman who was walking two poodles to jump aside. "Get in," he hollered to Hughes and took off before Hughes had a chance to close his door completely.

Halloran was excited and flushed, and he smiled at Hughes. He tore down Beacon Street and jumped onto Storrow Drive at the Arlington Street ramp. Veering around traffic, he ran the light at the junction of McGrath Highway and shot down into the southbound tunnel to the expressway. It was only when he had the vehicle moving in the fast lane that he turned to Hughes.

"We're on it, buddy boy," he said, settling in behind the wheel. "I picked them up about a half hour ago. They're driving a black Escalade. It was sitting in front of their place for an hour this morning and I stuck GPS on it. Easy as shit. I walked by, bent down and stuck it under the bumper with a magnet. Grab that laptop in the back seat and power it up. We should be able to see them on the road about twenty miles ahead of us."

Hughes reached behind and grabbed the gray laptop from the back seat, half hoping the technology would not work. He powered it up and looked at the icons that appeared on the blue screen.

"Click on the picture that says GPS," Halloran said.

"Will there be a record of this?" Hughes asked as a map filled the screen with a vivid green line and a slowly moving dot.

"When we're finished with this, that laptop will be at the bottom of the Atlantic."

Halloran drove fast, knowing that if he got stopped, he could badge the cop and get a pass. Hughes watched as they slowly gained on the blip on the screen.

After two hours, Hughes said, "They've stopped. Must be a rest area."

Halloran glanced at the dash gauges and said, "OK, we can stop right behind them. We'll fuel up now and eyeball our prey."

The rest area was a chaotic jumble of summer vacationers in packed SUVs. Halloran pulled into the back of the crowded lot and swung around slowly. They spotted the Escalade in the second row, sandwiched between a pickup and a BMW.

"There it is," Halloran whispered. "Let's get some gas and keep our eye on them."

When the tank was filled, Halloran maneuvered the car to the rear of the lot where they could see the Escalade four rows away. The parking lot shimmered in the heat. After about ten minutes they watched two men approach the Escalade, each in oversize shirts and workout pants. They each held a McDonald's bag. The bigger of the two had a large black gear bag slung crossways over his shoulders.

"See that?" Halloran said. "That's our money. They were afraid to leave it in the car."

"Shit," Hughes muttered. "They look bad ass."

"Nothing we can't handle," Halloran replied.

They watched as the two men sat in the big SUV for several minutes, finally tossing a couple of drink cups out the windows and heading back onto Route 95 south. Counting out two minutes, Halloran and Hughes started out behind them.

The Escalade rolled at a constant speed, with Halloran and Hughes running about a mile behind; the large luxury vehicle a moving red dot on the laptop as Hughes watched. Just below New Haven, the GPS showed them turning right and then left onto the Merritt Parkway. Crossing the New York State line, traffic grew thick and the Escalade's speed dropped to under sixty miles an hour. Hughes cautioned Halloran, who adjusted accordingly. They followed the Cadillac west on the Cross County Parkway toward Yonkers.

"Looks like they know where they are going, " Hughes said, stretching in his seat.

"Yeah." Halloran glanced over at the laptop Hughes was holding. "I'll bet we are getting close."

Hughes again felt the anxiety grow in the pit of his stomach. Then he saw the red dot turn off the roadway and stop. They took the same exit, just off the Cross County Shopping Center. Within two hundred feet of the exit, they drove past the North County Motel and saw the Escalade parked in front, the two men getting out.

"Don't look," Halloran warned. "Look straight ahead so they don't see you looking at them. We'll get ourselves in a place where we can sit and watch."

Turning around, Halloran saw a closed service station and pulled into the lot. They were a good five hundred yards away, but had a partial line of site to the black SUV. Halloran turned off the car and settled back, rubbing the back of his neck. Hughes stepped out and stretched his legs.

"OK, now we wait," Halloran said. "See that diner down the road? Go and get a couple of coffees and some goodies. If they start to move, I'll call and pick you up on the road."

Hughes was back quickly with a bag of donuts and two coffees. They settled down to wait, slouched low in the car. Halloran watched occasionally with a small pair of high-powered binoculars. Traffic bustled by fast and no one seemed to notice their car.

Time shouldered by in a slow crawl. Halloran dosed off while Hughes stared vacantly at the motel and the SUV parked outside. Dusk settled softly without any movement. Around seven o'clock, Hughes saw the two men emerge from their room. He elbowed Halloran, "They just came out." Halloran was instantly alert. As the Escalade pulled out, Halloran started the car, ready to follow. He waited until he saw them pull out of the parking lot and merge into traffic. As he was about to pull the car into gear, they saw the Escalade pull into the diner lot, three hundred feet down the road. "Lazy bastards," Halloran muttered.

They waited and watched for another forty minutes, until the two men emerged, climbing back into their SUV. Again, Halloran started the car, only to see them pull back into the motel lot and head back into Room 17.

Night rolled in. Hughes had his head back against the support while Halloran sipped his third coffee. He tossed the cup out the window and yawned. Then he saw the door to number 17 open and he elbowed Hughes. Halloran peered through his binoculars and watched as the two men carried two black duffel bags to the back of the Escalade. They tossed them in the back, looked around and then climbed into the cab. "Here we go, buddy boy," Halloran said, and started the car. "Stay on the GPS. It's going to be tough to follow in the traffic." They headed down the Major Deegan, rolling under a ribbon of lights. Hughes watched the dot on the screen heading south just under the speed limit.

"Looks like they're going into Manhattan. " Hughes said. Halloran nodded and concentrated on his driving. "Maybe you should speed up so they don't get too far ahead." Halloran nodded again without comment, and added another five miles an hour, pulling into the fast lane. They continued toward the Triborough Bridge, then Hughes exclaimed, "They're turning toward the East Side Drive." Traffic grew heavier and slower, Halloran weaving through expertly. Then they were on the East Side Drive moving south, approximately three hundred yards behind.

"Where do you figure they're going?" Hughes asked. Halloran didn't answer and Hughes looked over him. Halloran's expression was frozen in a grimace, both hands on the wheel. Hughes felt the tension rising off him like heat from a fire. On their right, the city was blinking awake for the night, with all its sophistication and energy. Full night descended. They continued on, veering through traffic, Hughes watching the computer in his lap, Halloran driving. As they approached downtown, Hughes announced, "They're getting off."

The dot on Hughes's laptop turned right, then right again and headed over the Williamsburg Bridge. "They're going over the bridge into Brooklyn," Hughes said.

"Figures," muttered Halloran. "Going into the snake pit."

After a series of lefts and rights, the dot came to a stop. Halloran and Hughes had gotten turned around and were trying to work their way to the Escalade. Finally, they drove past and realized the big SUV had pulled into a three story parking garage. It was perfect for a meeting. Out of the way, in a worn industrial area, unlit and with no foot traffic of anyone sane. Hughes looked at his watch and saw that it was almost ten o'clock. "What time do you think the meet would be?"

"How the fuck should I know," Halloran rasped back, clearly on edge. "We'll get out of the way and wait."

"That's all we've done. Wait." Hughes said.

"We'll be busy soon enough. Be ready to go when I say," Halloran said. They parked a block and a half away, behind a white van gone to rust with its tires removed on one side. They sat in complete darkness and watched rats scamper around the garbage cans. An hour later, a pickup pulled in, followed by a black Lexus. "That's it. It's going down." Halloran said, sitting up straight. "Did you see Florida plates on either of those?"

"I think the pickup did," Hughes responded.

"OK, unless we hear gun shots, we can figure it's gone down. We tail the pickup. Let's hope they're tired and don't pick us out." Both men felt an adrenaline rush like a hot dart shoot through their spines.

Chapter 19

The top floor of the decrepit garage was empty except for the hulking black SUV, backed into a corner. The cement floor was cracked and stained black from rain and soot. The parking lines had long disappeared. The glitter of Manhattan could be seen across the tar rooftops. The pickup and Lexus drove slowly to the top floor, and parked twenty feet across from the black Escalade. Ciracero and Toady sat for a minute, trying to watch both cars. Toady pulled a Glock from under the seat and held it at his side. Both men were tired from the trip, but still alert. All three vehicles sat clicking and cooling for a moment.

Then a large man emerged from the back of the Lexus. Despite the summer warmth, he was wearing a black pea coat and black jeans. He walked over to the pickup. Ciracero rolled the driver's window down halfway as he approached.

"How ya doin?" he said through the window.

"We looking good?" was the reply.

"We're ready to do business," Ciracero said. Toady shifted in his seat.

The man in black turned back toward the Lexus and gave a thumbs-up. At this point, the two men from the

Escalade emerged and stood next to their car. Toady climbed out of the truck to stand behind the bed, peering over at the men, now three of them walking toward him. Ciracero got out of the truck and spoke to the men, now standing in front of him. He held his hands out in front of him.

"Three mil each. We have the product." At this point, another man climbed out of the Lexus, carrying a large black canvas bag. One of the men from the Escalade held a large canvas bag as well. Both bags were placed next to the pickup and Ciracero, his heart pounding, unzipped each and peered inside.

"We operate on trust. I believe you do also," he said, then pulled the bags toward him and nodded to Toady, who went around to the back of the truck with his steel bar. With a loud bang, the false bottom popped up. Inside were the neatly wrapped bricks of cocaine. A man in a dark blue workout jacket stepped up and pulled out a switch blade knife. He quickly slipped a brick from the lower stack and scooped out a small amount. He stepped back behind his car and knelt down. From a small gym bag he pulled out some chemical paraphernalia and did some quick experiments. Standing, he nodded to the men. Someone said, "Go." Ciracero gingerly stepped forward and picked up one of the black canvas bags. Again looking inside, he heaved in into the cab of the truck, behind the seats. As he did so, the others started unloading the bricks of cocaine. It was quickly split up between the two factions, New York and Boston. Each filled the trunks with the bricks while Ciracero grabbed the second bag and threw it beside the first. Within six or seven minutes, the deal was complete.

Ciracero, now feeling more confident, said, "Nice

doing business, gentlemen. We're heading back. Enjoy." With that, he nodded to Toady who was still standing on the other side of the pickup, his gun at his side. They climbed into the truck, Ciracero shaking almost uncontrollably as the adrenaline wore off. He started the vehicle and jerkily drove to the exit ramp and out of the garage. Toady turned around in his seat and looked in both bags. Each was filled with banded hundred dollar bills, three million in each bag. "Holy shit," he exclaimed. "We fuckin did it."

Ciracero wiped his brow with the back of his hand and tried to find his way out of Brooklyn. He turned the wrong way down a one-way street, but luckily there was no oncoming traffic. Finally seeing a sign for the Williamsburg Bridge, he swung onto the access road and onto the bridge proper. The lights of Manhattan spread out to the right like an immense diamond necklace. Ciracero suddenly felt exhausted. "I'm fucking beat. We gotta stop and get some shut eye," he said. Toady nodded as he stared out the window, his gun still on his lap.

Chapter 20

Parked in the shadows a half block up the street from the garage, hidden by the rusting van, Halloran and Hughes waited for their prey. The wait had been silent for the most part. Halloran seemed to be in deep thought, and Hughes was having major reservations. Neither was in the mood for talking. Suddenly, movement near the garage door startled them. The pickup they had been waiting for pulled out of the bay and sped away.

"That's it," said Halloran excitedly. "Let's go." Hughes reached out and grasped the grab handle. Halloran quickly maneuvered onto the road and started after the truck, being careful to stay a block behind. "Keep your eye on them. We can't lose them now." The pickup turned down a one-way street, heading in the wrong direction.

"Shit," Halloran said. "Hold on." He accelerated to the next block, turned hard and floored the SUV up the parallel street, stopping short at the stop sign at the end, just as the truck drove out and onto the boulevard. He paused a moment, and then drove out, letting a car get in between.

"Grab the binoculars," Halloran said. Hughes reached behind him into a small leather bag and pulled out the pair of gyro binoculars.

"Got them," Hughes said, looking through the thick optical gear. The binoculars steadied the image and Hughes could clearly see the truck some sixty yards ahead.

"Don't lose them," Halloran commanded, both hands on the wheel and a grit hard grimace on his face. The pickup merged into the right lane up the East Side Drive. Traffic was thick, but moving at a steady pace. Halloran and Hughes tailed, keeping a car or two in between. Hughes held the binoculars to his face, giving Halloran an ongoing narrative of the truck's movements, more to steady his nerves than to keep Halloran posted.

Inside the pickup, fatigue was settling on the two men like thick tar. Ciracero was sweating heavily and Toady placed his gun in the glove box, leaned back in the seat and closed his eyes. All they had to do now was drive at a reasonable pace south and complete the payoff. Ciracero was thinking about his commission.

Toady, with his eyes closed, whispered, "Ever think about keeping the load in back for ourselves?"

Ciracero glanced over. "Asshole, don't even think about it. They would hunt you down and you would be lucky if all they did was kill you. We'll do our job and keep our mouths shut. I'll forget you ever said that."

Ciracero saw the sign for the Willis Avenue Bridge and followed it, headed for the George Washington Bridge. Halloran and Hughes realized immediately where they were going.

"Christ, they're heading south already," Hughes said.

"Don't think they can go far," Halloran replied. "My snitch said they were supposed to drive straight through from Miami. If that's the case, they've been on the road for days and can't go on forever."

New York spread out below like a living colossus as

they drove across the bridge. The truck bumped heavily along on the broken road. Toady said, "I'm fuckin beat. Need some bacon and eggs and shut eye. Pull over someplace so we can crash."

Ciracero rubbed his eyes and shrugged. "We're supposed to stop for nothing," he said.

"Bullshit. You're falling asleep behind the wheel. Stop someplace."

On the right, a pink neon sign glared, Bridge View Motel. Ciracero slowed down to get a better look and said, "OK. We'll get about four hours. There's a diner next door. After we check in and secure the merchandise, go over there and get some food to go."

Some hundred yards behind, lost in the sea of headlights, Halloran and Hughes saw the pickup slow and stop in front of the motel. "There it is," Halloran exclaimed. Hughes felt the pit in his stomach grow. "Let's get around quick and see what room they're in."

With that, he accelerated to the next exit and came back on the opposite side of the roadway, telling Hughes to watch the men. Hughes brought the binoculars up and saw the two men, each carrying a large duffel bag, approach the third room on the left side of the motel. The smaller of the two opened the door and they both went in. Halloran drove to the next exit and made a U-turn, pulling into the motel lot on the right, just as the large man lumbered toward the diner next door.

Hughes could feel the perspiration on his forehead, and he noticed that his hands were shaking. "Jesus, you sure about this, Bill?"

"Are you kidding? We are on the verge of changing our lives for good. Relax and follow my lead," Halloran said in a whisper.

As Hughes watched, the big man, a rumbling buffalo, headed for the diner. "He's gone for food," Hughes said. "Something we should do," he muttered to himself.

Then he turned to Halloran, putting down the binoculars. "I don't like the feel of this. I vote to head home and talk about it over a beer."

Halloran gave him a look. "Danny, this is no time to crap out on me. Just follow my lead and we'll be in and out in a nanosecond. I've figured all the angles."

Hughes brought the binoculars back up to his face. "Before I walk into something I don't understand, tell me again how you've got this figured out."

"OK. Like I said, those assholes are stupid. We go in hard and fast. They're tired and not thinking. They'll never know what hit them. We grab the bags and bolt. As we leave, I tell them Mousey Miranda says thank you. Hopefully they will spot the New York plates on the car, too."

"Who the hell is Mousey Miranda?" Hughes watched the big man return from the diner, carrying a large takeout bag. A dim light flashed from the motel room door as he knocked three times and the door opened.

"He's a dumb shit wannabe who tries to play all sides. He's already suspected by us for two different hits, from two different families. I'll even dump some cash in his pitiful bank account. That will really fuck him up. Let's hope they don't believe he's innocent after they grab and torture him. I figure we're doing society several favors. Then we lay low and wait a little before living the good life."

Hughes was quiet for a moment. He sat looking out the windshield at nothing. Then, he said, "OK, let's do it."

Halloran smiled at him. He got out of the SUV, opened the back and pulled out a duffel bag. From it he pulled out two shotguns, the barrels sawed off to four inches, two ski masks, and a hydraulic battering ram. He handed Hughes a shotgun and several plastic ties. "Take these to tie them up. Do not say a word. I'll do all the talking. Ready?"

Hughes nodded. They stood silently, looking around. Seeing no one, they headed toward the door to the motel room. The white noise of the highway cloaked the crunch of their footsteps across the parking lot. High lamps at the corners of the lot gave off an orange glow. Hughes anxiously looked over his shoulder as they approached the room. He saw this moment as a passage to another life, good or bad.

They stopped at the door and Halloran calmly looked around. Cars scattered in the lot sat like cold boxes, silent and inert. No one was around. The highway was distant and removed. Halloran nodded and burst into action, smashing the door with his battering ram. It blew off the hinges. He rushed in, screaming at them to get down and brandishing his shotgun. Hughes had no choice but to follow, his gun held high. Inside, the two men were sitting on the bed among scattered food containers. They stared in uncomprehending confusion. Ciracero had a piece of chicken in his hand, which he continued to grip as he threw his hands up.

Toady stood up quickly and took a step forward. Halloran lunged at him and smashed the butt of the shotgun into his nose, shattering it instantly. Blood and small pieces of bone gushed from the man's face. It was like lightning exploded in the room. Hughes saw the two black bags stacked against the nightstand and went for them. He hefted one onto his shoulder and pushed the other toward Halloran, who made no move to grab it.

"Welcome to New York, assholes," he said. "Mousey appreciates your visit."

"Who the. . . what the. . ." Ciracero said, as he started to stand, the chicken drumstick still in his hand. Toady was on the floor, holding both hands to his nose, trying to stop the flowing blood. Halloran smiled, hefted his gun to chest level and aimed it at Ciracero's chest. He pulled the trigger. The blast shook the cheap room and blew a ragged hole in Ciracero's chest, catapulting him across the room where he collapsed against the wall, eyes wide open and staring, before going dim. The blood sprayed out on the bed and carpet. Hughes's ears rang to the point of deafness. He looked at Halloran in horror and disbelief. Halloran bent and picked up the other bag, backing out of the room. "Let's go," he snarled.

Hughes was frozen for an instant, and then he backed out behind Halloran. Toady sat bleeding and gawking at the awkwardly bent body of Ciracero.

Outside, Halloran sprinted for the car, lugging the heavy bag that banged against his leg. Hughes, bending under the weight of the one he was carrying, followed behind as quickly as he could. When he got to the car, Halloran had the back open and his bag inside. He jumped into the driver's seat and yelled, "Move!" to Hughes. Hughes jammed his bag into the back, slammed the door down and almost didn't make it into the passenger seat as Halloran began to speed out of the lot heading east.

Inside the car was silent except for the strain of the engine. Hughes was in shock. After a minute, he looked over at Halloran who was driving intensely, both hands tightly holding the steering wheel. "What the fuck did you do?"

Halloran said nothing. He slowed to merge with the

traffic, moving into the middle lane. The air in the car was thick with perspiration.

Hughes felt nauseous. The bile was rising up into the back of his mouth. His hands were shaking. Looking out the passenger window, he said, almost in a whisper. "You just killed a man. Why?"

Halloran relaxed enough to look to him. "We had to make a statement," he said. "Only bad guys would do that. They will never suspect good guys did it. Besides, we did the world a favor. One less scumbag."

"You asshole. You never told me you were going to do that. It's insane."

"Look, if I told you I was thinking about it, would you have come?" The lights of the Tudor style houses they passed along the parkway shone with indifferent innocence. Hughes could not help but think of the people in the houses, normal families, living without violence, their problems routine.

Halloran chuckled. It was a release. "We did it, dude. No fucking idea how much is in those bags, but I'll bet it's enough." He swung the car north on the Merritt Parkway. At the first rest stop, he pulled the car in and swung to the left in the L-shaped parking lot. There were no cars along the far row, which bordered dark woods. The car was not visible from the parkway. Hughes realized Halloran had scoped out the parking lot previously, and began to realize how much had been pre-planned, including the murder of one of the couriers. He felt somehow used and violated.

Halloran shut the car off and sat quietly for a minute, only the white noise of the adjacent parkway and the clicking of the cooling engine audible. Then he got out of the car and pulled out several black garbage bags from the back. He took off his jacket and shoes and stuffed them into a bag, putting on a flannel shirt and new sneakers. He walked around to the passenger side of the car, opened the door and handed a bag to Hughes. "Danny, put your stuff in this, I've got a change for you in the back. There's a river a little bit north. I'm going to weigh down the bags and dump the shotgun in it. We'll be clean." Hughes, in a semi-stupor, complied. When they pulled off the road at the river, neither man looked in the two canvas bags in the back. It was like they could not accept the past two hours.

They pulled into Boston four hours later. Halloran piloted the SUV up Beacon Hill and the leafy Mt. Vernon Street and then to Joy Street. The late August air hung heavy and oppressive. The car nosed toward the Boston Common, which looked deserted and pristine. He pulled to the curb and turned to look at Hughes, who stared at the greenery below.

"It will be better tomorrow and every day after. Take a bag out and hide it in your place. Tell no one, especially not Angie."

Hughes got out without a word and walked to the back of the car. The bags looked to Hughes like two black tumors. After a minute, he looked up and down the short, narrow street and, seeing no one, pulled a bag out and walked into the silent building. Halloran pulled away from the curb and drove slowly down Beacon Street.

Hughes struggled the bag up to his apartment and pushed it into a closet, throwing his ski jacket on top of it. He had no desire to look inside. Pulling off his t-shirt, he walked into the bedroom and sat on the edge of the bed, staring out into space. His hands were shaking and he felt like he was going to throw up. After several minutes, he got up and poured himself four ounces of scotch from the bottle he had stashed in the kitchen cabinet. He drank it down neat and returned to the bedroom, lying down and finally falling into a haunted sleep.

Chapter 21

Halloran drove in light traffic to the South Shore. His house was dark as he pulled into the garage. He got out of the car and looked outside for any kind of movement. Satisfied, he pulled the garage door closed and found a flashlight in the clutter of his workbench. Opening the back, he pulled the bag out and let it drop heavily on the floor. He unzipped it and looked inside with the light.

"Jesus fuckin Christ," he muttered to himself. The bag was filled with hundred dollar bills, bound in thick stacks with rubber bands. More money than he had ever seen before. A shiver went through his body.

He zipped the bag closed and hauled it to the far corner, where he crammed it into a black metal cabinet, taking out one wad of bills. He covered it with a plastic tarp and locked the cabinet. He placed his chain saw in front of it. Stepping back, he was satisfied it was hidden well enough until he could figure out a better spot. He then closed and locked the garage door and went around the rambling ranch house to the back door. Unlocking it quietly, he stepped into the unlit kitchen. As he closed the door, the lights came on, startling him enough that he reached for his side arm. Sitting at the kitchen table, a coffee mug in front of her, was Laura. "Sneaking in?" she said.

"Christ, you scared the shit out of me. What are you doing sitting in the dark?"

"Waiting for my dear husband to find his way home." The acid in her tone cut sharply. "Out on an important case?"

"Yeah. What the fuck do you think?" Halloran stepped to the sink and started washing his hands.

"You probably ought to wash something else," she said.

"What the hell is that supposed to mean? You accusing me of something?" He tossed the dish towel onto the counter as he dried his hands and started walking out of the kitchen.

"I'm sick and tired of you catting around. Some bimbo called here tonight looking for you. It's one thing when you can't keep it in your pants when you are out, but bringing it into our house is too much."

"Come off it, Laura, you know I'm working all kinds of cases. Get off my back."

"Maybe I'll get off your back permanently," she said, getting up so fast the coffee mug went sailing off the table, shattering on the floor.

Halloran stood staring at her for a minute, then said, "Fuck you. I'm going to bed."

"Not in my bed, you're not. Keep your bimbo stink in the spare room."

"That's what I want to do." He strode out of the kitchen and down the hall to the guest room, slamming the door behind him.

Chapter 22

The next day was September 1st, with Labor Day weekend looming three days ahead. Somehow, as if nature flipped a switch, the air cooled, hinting at the impending autumn. Dan Hughes woke to the ringing of his cell phone, which was in the pocket of the pants he was still wearing. He had sweated through his clothes and was as clammy as if he had not slept in two days. He fumbled for the phone, confused. He answered on the fourth ring.

Angie was perky. "Hi, handsome. Sleeping in? Must be nice to be a man of leisure."

Hughes was silent for a minute. "Hello, Angie. Had a bad night."

"Anything I can help with?"

"I don't want to talk now. Can I call you later?" Hughes asked. The events of the past evening were weighing heavily on him. He hung up and held his head in his hands. "Asshole Halloran," he muttered to himself.

He got up, shuffled into the kitchen, and put coffee on. The clothes he wore from the night before hung on him like a confession. What was his status? Accessory to murder was the least of where he thought he stood. He wanted no part of this and couldn't believe how Halloran had sucked him in. Hughes paced the kitchen, unable to think clearly. He kept visualizing the blood spraying out and exploding like a tomato in front of him. He walked to the window and looked down on Joy Street. Young couples walked happily together, unburdened by guilt. Trees hung heavy with the late summer foliage and the world outside seemed carefree. He made his way slowly over to the closet. The bag sat inside like a huge black leech. He slid it out, surprised again by its heaviness. Standing over it, he felt a shiver run through him. He bent and unzipped it and stared silently down at the wads of cash. He felt strangely indifferent and shoved the bag back into the closet. He walked back to the bedroom, pulled the curtains shut and lay down on the bed.

His fitful sleep was interrupted by Angie's arrival. She called out to him as she came into the bedroom. He sat up, groggy and disorientated.

"Christ, Danny. You look like shit," she said.

He shook off the sleep that clung to him like a thick fungus. "Bad night, Angie. Couldn't sleep," he said. "I'm better now."

She looked at him silently for a minute. "You all right?" she asked.

He thought about what had happened and desperately wanted to tell her about it, but couldn't. "Yeah, I'm ok. Let me get into the shower and get some coffee in me."

He washed off the tiredness, but not the dread. Angie made coffee and handed a cup and a towel to him as he stepped out of the shower. "You want to tell me what's up?" she asked.

He sipped the coffee and thought for a moment. "Nothing much. Just worked a case with Bill. Nothing came of it," he finally replied.

"Danny, there is a lot of you in me. Let's talk." Angie walked him back into the kitchen, the towel wrapped around his waist. She searched the refrigerator for breakfast food and found some Jimmy Dean sausage and rye bread. She started frying up the sausage, eyeing him warily as he sipped his coffee.

Hughes stood up and walked into the bedroom, pulling on a pair of jeans he found on the floor. He grabbed a t-shirt from his dresser drawer and yanked it over his head, the effort giving him time to think. No way could he involve Angie. He knew she would be horrified and, with her temper, feared she would walk out for good. Returning to the kitchen, he saw the small breakfast Angie had cooked him sitting on the table like an oversized communion offering. Angie leaned against the stove, concerned and confused. She was quiet while he ate. After a while, she said, "Danny, do you want me to leave?"

"I don't know. I'm not in a good mood. Maybe it's best if I'm alone for a while."

She looked at him hard. "OK. Call me if you feel like it." She got up and walked out without another word.

Hughes sat at the table for a minute, then went back to the closet and looked inside. Then he quickly shut the door and locked it with the old skeleton key that was in the keyway. He went back to the bedroom and lay down again, lost in thought.

Chapter 23

The house in Sunny Isles was lit up like a garish tropical Christmas tree. There were two hulking SUVs with blacked out windows in the drive, and a sleek thirty-six foot Trojan rocking peacefully at the dock. Inside, Tessio was talking louder than usual.

Lounging on the silk couch opposite him was Pauley DeMarco, new to Miami. He was wearing white cotton pants and a nylon warm-up jacket. Standing at the bar in front of the window looking out to the Intercoastal was Bennie Silvio and Georgie Escobar, two soldiers from Lauderdale. Tessio's face was scarlet and spittle sprayed from his mouth as he spoke.

"Find out who the fuck grabbed our fucking money and kill them and get the money back. I don't trust that fucking Toady. How the fuck did he survive and a good guy like Ciracero get clipped?" he said to the group. No one replied. "Call everyone you know. What about that buddy of Ciracero's? What the fuck is his name? Horse shit or something like that."

"Hornez," said DeMarco. "They call him the horse."

"Get him over here and see if knows anything. Maybe

Ciracero suspected something," Tessio said. He was still red as a radish and puffing like an overheated teapot.

Phone calls were made and Hornez showed up at the house two hours later. Everyone except Tessio was showing the effects of the two bottles of scotch and the bottle of rum they had emptied. Hornez came into the house like he was walking the green mile. Tessio told him to sit down and then rolled his immense body in front of him. "What the fuck do you know about us getting ripped off in New York?" The words spewed out like a machine gun.

Hornez stared back, confused. He was silent, then said, "What? I don't know anything about it."

Tessio's eyes were snakelike. "If that fuck Ciracero said anything to anybody about our deal, I have to know. What did he tell you?"

"All he said was that he was helping with a big deal and was looking forward to a big commission." The sweat was accumulating on his upper lip.

"So, who the fuck did you tell?" Tessio hissed.

Hornez stood and stared. "No one," he said.

"Gimme your phone," Tessio said. Hornez pulled it out of his pocket and held it out. Tessio grabbed it and tossed it to DeMarco, who was sitting half drunk and amused on the couch. He missed the catch and the phone landed on the floor in front of him with a bang. "Johnnie Damon," Tessio said to DeMarco. "Pick it up and see if there are any New York numbers in it." DeMarco fumbled with the phone for several agonizing minutes, and finally said, "I don't see nothing."

"Any numbers that look funny?" Tessio asked.

"There are a couple that look like they are out of the country, some 617 numbers, and a couple in the 781 area." DeMarco said, scrolling through the phone.

"Write them down. We can check them later. Give him back the fucking phone." DeMarco tossed it back to Hornez, who caught it and slipped it back into his pocket, trying to cover up his trembling hand. "OK, Horseman," Tessio breathed. "You hear anything you call me right away. We will get those fuckers."

Hornez walked outside and got into his Mustang. He felt his stomach heave and drove away as fast as possible so as to not dirty the lawn.

Chapter 24

Halloran navigated his new Lexus around the corner and down his street, past the darkened houses set back from their manicured lawns. He bumped over the rock at the corner of his driveway and pulled into the garage, stopping just before banging into the back wall. Turning off the car, he chuckled to himself. He got out, looked around slyly then closed the garage door. He moved to the cabinet that sat in the far corner, picked up the case off the workbench that held a handsaw and pulled out the key stuck under the blade. Opening the cabinet, he pulled out the canvas sack. He unzipped it and peered inside. Smiling, he pulled out a wad of bills and stuffed them into his jacket pocket. He put the satchel back inside, re-locked the cabinet and hid the key back under the saw blade. He turned and strode out of the garage, tripping slightly over a big wheel tricycle before silently letting himself into the house. Keeping the lights off, he stopped and listened for anything stirring, then took a few steps forward. Laura's voice came as shrill as a drill bit on a metal sheet.

"Nice of you to come home. I suppose you were working until 3 a.m. again?" the sarcasm clear in her voice.

Halloran stopped short, turned and flicked on the

light. She was sitting in the dark, dressed and obviously waiting. He tried to focus through his scotch haze and realized this was a confrontation. He was in no mood.

"Fuck you," he said. "I'm working so you can buy the shit you want."

"My ass, you're working. You reek of booze and sex. Don't insult me."

He stood without replying then turned toward the master bedroom.

"Don't turn your back on me," she screamed. "Are you a husband or a drunken whore master?"

He kept going without a word, pulling his clothes off as he went, falling into bed with just his shirt on. Within minutes, Laura heard his deep snoring. She got up and looked through the glass paned door into the garage, just as she had done when Halloran drove in. In the dim moonlight through the window, she had seen him walk to the corner of the garage, and watched the shadow of his bulk moving around there. She knew he was up to something. She stood thinking. The night was quiet except for the faint nasal vibrations coming from the bedroom. She opened the door quietly and slipped inside the garage. The engine of the gleaming SUV was still crackling from its heat. With only the faint light from the window, she made her way around the car to the corner where she had seen her husband standing. She saw the metal cabinet squeezed into the corner and tried its door, only to find it solidly locked. She looked around for a key, but could hardly see anything in the dark and did not want to risk turning on a light in case Halloran woke up. Something didn't feel right to her and she decided to examine the garage more closely the next time he was out.

Chapter 25

anny Hughes was trying to live normally. He had not touched the black bag, which remained locked in his closet like a sleeping serpent. Business in the week following the rip-off was fairly busy, which helped keep his mind off what had happened, but he moved through each day in a gray cloud. The clutter in his head came alive at night like evil demons, making real sleep impossible. Angie had called several times, but he let it go to voicemail to avoid her. A light but steady drizzle outside hinted at the coming fall season. He gazed out his window at the umbrellas springing up and moving down Beacon Street like brightly colored mushrooms. He made coffee, but had no appetite for food. He pulled on a pair of jeans and stayed barefoot and shirtless. A stack of mail was piling up on his desk and he forced himself to sit down and face it.

By noon, the drizzle had beefed up to real rain, which pounded outside his open window. It reflected his mood. The sound of a key in the front door startled him into a defensive attitude. Quickly getting up, he saw Angie come in. She was wearing tight jeans and a white t-shirt under a Red Sox windbreaker. Her hair was wet, bringing out curls. She had the kind of beauty that you didn't notice at first, but would make you stop to turn around and look again. Hughes didn't want to talk to her, but was inwardly glad to see her.

"OK, hot shot, why are you ducking me?" she said with a hint of anger in her voice.

"Been busy," Hughes whispered back. He faced her, then turned back to his desk.

Angie looked appraisingly at him, confused but glad she had come over. Even as sullen as he was, she still felt that physical longing for him. He sat back down, his back to her. She waited, then walked over and lightly placed her hands on his bare shoulders and started a tenuous massage.

"Stop," he said. She backed away.

"What the fuck is your problem?" she said, her anger growing.

Turning toward her, Hughes said, "Nothing. What the fuck is your problem?"

"Goddamn it, Danny, if you are dumping me, just fucking say so."

He was silent for a minute. "Angie, I'm not dumping you or anything like that. It's just I've got a lot on my mind."

She turned away and helped herself to a cup of coffee from the small kitchen. Turning back to him she said, "OK, want to talk about it?"

Hughes got up and stared out the window. Even in the rain, the few pedestrians he saw seemed to have no worries. "Angie, just leave me alone. I've got some problems to work out."

"Leave you alone?" Her voice rising. "We've been together, what, two, three years. We have personal secrets in the vault and you want me to leave you alone when you have an issue?" She turned and poured herself more coffee. It helped settle her down.

"You're not my mother, just a girlfriend. I don't have to tell you everything that's on my mind."

"What am I, just a good fuck once in a while? I thought we had something special, something deeper." Her voice was shaking from anger and hurt.

"Look, I don't mean it that way, it's just something you should not get involved in." He realized he didn't mean to say it that way, and tried to back off a little.

"If you haven't noticed, I am involved." Her anger was overcoming the hurt. "If we can't confide in each other, what do we have? Some fun and games?"

Hughes spoke louder. "Just fucking leave me alone. It's none of your business." He sat back down at his desk, not looking at her.

She stood staring, a feeling of shock and remorse coming over her. After a minute, she found nothing more to say and stormed out of the apartment, slamming the door behind her. Hughes sat staring at the wall for several long minutes, then walked over to the closet and unlocked the door. The black bag was still there, promise and menace at the same time.

The phone rang. Before he could say hello, he heard Halloran. "Meet me at the Bristol at six o'clock. We should talk." He hung up. Outside the warm rain increased, the air was heavy with moisture.

Chapter 26

T he bar at the Four Seasons felt like money. Sounds were muted as Hughes walked up the three stairs to the thickly carpeted lounge. Couples and powerful men were scattered around at small tables. On the right side of the long bar Hughes saw Halloran chatting with a blonde in a very short, black dress. Her hair was a bright yellow and hung straight to her shoulders. Halloran was leaning toward her with a sly smile on his face, his belly fat obvious under his shirt. Hughes was certain he was looking down the front of her dress.

Walking up next to them, he said, "Hey, Bill."

Halloran turned to him, grinning, "Hi, partner. Meet Kimberly. She works over at the Danielle Modeling Agency. "Kim, say hello to my buddy, Danny."

Kimberly looked at Hughes with large, deep blue eyes, heavily etched with mascara. "Hi, Danny," she said in a flirtatious manner. Her look had an effect. Hughes mumbled his reply.

Halloran turned back to the bartender, who was standing discreetly away polishing crystal. The back of the bar sparkled with an impressive array of bottles, familiar and exotic. Halloran pointed to his and the woman's glasses and ordered a Johnnie Walker Blue for Hughes. The bartender placed the drinks on clean cocktails napkins in front of them and retreated to the far end of the bar. Halloran drank half of his in one gulp and put his hand on Kimberly's thigh. She ignored it and continued talking to him about her girlfriend who had been abandoned by her date in Mexico. Hughes sipped his drink, being ignored. Finally Halloran said to her, "Honey, Danny and I have some business, give us a couple of minutes."

She looked at Hughes, gave him a devastating smile and slipped off her barstool. She took a last sip of her Cosmopolitan, kissed Halloran on the cheek and strode off, a slight sway to her very watchable bottom.

"Hughes looked at Halloran with disgust. "Christ, Bill. We were supposed to be discreet. You're here wearing a ten thousand dollar watch, drinking fifty-dollar scotch and fucking around with a bimbo. What kind of low profile is that?"

"Easy Danny boy." Halloran was grinning foolishly at Hughes. ""I'm being careful and no one will notice anything. Maybe you should live a little. You look like shit."

"We were going to wait at least a year. What's it been, a week?"

Halloran continued to grin. "How's it going with Angie? Man, that babe is hot."

Hughes looked at him for a long minute. "She's OK. I haven't been talking much to her." Two women in short summer dresses glided by, catching Halloran's attention. He watched them seat themselves at the far end of the bar before turning back to Hughes.

"What?" he said, refocusing on Hughes. Then, "Laura's giving me shit. It's been building a long time, but

I'm really getting fed up with her. I didn't want to make a move because of the kids, but I've had it."

"What are you telling me?" Hughes asked. "Are you splitting up? Is there anything else you can do to draw attention to yourself?"

"I've got to do what I've got to do. There's hardly any agent in the office that hasn't been through a divorce or two. I'm the exception."

"What's this got to do with me?" Danny asked. Halloran circled his finger over his glass, signaling another round to the bartender. The drinks were poured instantly. He waited for the bartender to walk away before answering.

"I've got to use a little of the money to set up an apartment for myself. But, I don't want you to worry. I'll be discreet."

"You're being as discreet as a naked woman in church. I won't touch my share, maybe ever. I don't need you to suck me into anything further. I haven't slept since that night and can't get over what you did."

Halloran grinned more. "I did it for us both. We're clear like I told you."

Hughes stood up and looked Halloran over, noticing the roll of belly fat under the wrinkled white shirt and the lack of a crease in his pants. He shook his head slowly. "Bill, stay the fuck away from me," and he turned and walked away. Halloran watched him leave then signaled for another scotch.

Chapter 27

Tessio was sitting aft on the Hatteras, *Snow White*, his flowered shorts and sandals, making him look a little like an inverted flower barrel. One fat hand was holding his third Mojito, while the other waved around a six-inch Cuban cigar. Sweat ran down the hair on his chest like grease smears.

"Even I got pressure to get that dough back. We fuckin' got to do something," he said to no one in particular of the three men who sat looking at him. The marina in Fort Lauderdale was crammed with yachts resting quietly and empty on the hot September day.

"Everybody says it's New York; maybe Boston. They both deny doin' the rip off and I know those guys for a long time. Looks like them, but doesn't smell like them," he said.

The men, Dino, Charlie Big Hands and Randy Lambs, were Tessio's soldiers. They nodded as he spoke, but offered no response. He looked at their deadpan expressions and shook his head. "Anyone got any ideas?" he asked again.

Finally Randy spoke. "We got the phone from Ciracero's friend, what's his name, Horse? Maybe there's some call Ciracero made that will tell us how they found him."

"Jesus," Tessio said, again shaking his head at the amazing level of stupidity in front of him. "OK, look into the phone thing. And, I want every rock in New York and Boston turned over to find who the fuck ripped us off. I still can't figure out how anyone knew where they were." He looked at the shrugs from his crew. Then, "Did anyone wonder how that fuckin' Toad ended up with a bloody nose while Ciracero ended up with a hole in him the size of a lasagna pan? Charlie, you and Randy grab that asshole and wash him clean. He must be the rat."

Charlie Big Hands held his hands in front of him with his palms up. "We already worked on him, boss. Says he knows from nothin'."

"Work him again. I need answers. Dino, get me another fuckin' drink and come up with some bright ideas, you moron."

As Dino went into the galley, Randy pulled out Hornez's phone from his fanny pack and started scrolling through it. After a minute, he stopped and stared at it. "This is weird, there's a 617 number here," he said. "Where's that?"

Tessio looked at him in disbelief. "That's fuckin' Boston. What would he be calling Boston for? Maybe those punks up there have pulled a fast one. Call the fuckin' number and see who answers."

Halloran was just getting ready to leave his office when he heard the phone ring in his briefcase. He stared at it for a minute, then opened the case and pushed the answer button. He said nothing and listened. Dead air, then, "Who the fuck is this?" He held the phone away from his face, looked at it, and clicked it off. He stood silent for a while then closed his case, putting the phone in his pocket. He headed to the South Shore through Southie, stopping at the channel to drop the phone into the murky water.

On the *Snow White*, Dino also held a phone out and stared at it. "That was weird," he said to Tessio. "Someone answered, but said nothing."

Tessio drained his Mojito and said, "Call that fuckin' private eye we know. What's his name, Romeo? Get him to trace the number, fast. And, get that fuckin' Horsey or whatever his name is here. I smell some shit."

Chapter 28

Halloran was unsettled as he fought the traffic back to the South Shore. He was thinking, "*What the fuck, I haven't heard from him in four days and now it looks like he lost the phone. Dumb fuck.*"

The September sun hung low in the west, a pumpkin pie sitting just over the horizon, as the summer waned. He was driving his new Lexus LX, the smell of expensive leather still fresh. The car was so easy to drive that he could pay scant attention to it while he confronted his troubling thoughts. Losing a CI could be disastrous in many ways. The phone number led nowhere so that wasn't a big risk, but if that mope rolls over on him, it could start leading back. Not good. The Bureau could give him shit and start looking more closely, too. Not good. The worry was creeping up no matter how he tried to confirm his confidence in his perfect plan.

The Ninety Nine Restaurant featured decent, inexpensive food and good-sized drinks. More importantly, he would look perfectly at home with the after-work crowd there. He swung off Route 3 and pulled into the parking lot. An hour later, three Johnnie Walker Blacks and a plate of Buffalo wings had settled his nerves. He headed home, determined to shower and swing out again. He needed a little walking around money and was hoping Laura was out doing something inane, like she usually was, so he could grab some without her peeking around at him.

Her car was in the driveway as he pulled in past it and hit the remote to open the garage door. Closing the door behind him, he got out and listened for her. Satisfied she was not paying attention, he got out the key to the locker, unzipped the bag enough for his hand to fit inside and pulled out a wad of hundreds. Not bothering to count it, he re-locked the locker and walked into the kitchen from the side door.

Laura was sitting at the kitchen island, a glass of wine and a writing pad in front of her.

"Nice of you to show up," she said, tapping a pencil on the pad. "You home or just passing through again?"

Halloran pulled off his suit jacket and tossed it over a barstool. He looked in the refrigerator without answering. He turned back and caught the look in her eyes.

So, where are the kids?" he asked.

"At the Bryants. They don't need to see you or hear us."

He went to the sink and poured a glass of water and drank it down, some of it spilling down the front of his shirt. "What are you talking about?"

"I've had it. We have to talk. Now is as good a time as any."

"What's there to talk about? You have everything you want." He turned away, pulled out a bottle of scotch from the cupboard and poured a water glass half full.

"What you are doing right now is a good place to start. Most of the time, whenever you decide to come home, you reek of booze. And, I can smell women on you."

"You're crazy. There's no smell of women on me."

Her eyes were livid with rage. "You think I'm stupid. You're into something that's way over your head and you're acting like a complete asshole. I can't take it anymore. What the hell's happened to you?"

He poured more scotch into his glass, took a sip and glared at her. "I'm sick of all of this bullshit. You don't do anything but shop and bitch, you made the kids into monsters and you're dead weight in bed, the once a month you are in the mood. I don't need any of this."

"You don't need this? You think I do? Why don't you just get out? You're into something that I don't want to know about. Get out!"

Halloran looked at her over his glass. He suppressed a smile and said, "I'll be back for my things. We can talk again when you're rational and not a bitch."

Laura picked up and threw the writing pad at him. It fluttered harmlessly to the floor. "Get out!" she screamed in frustration.

He turned away and walked back through the side door into the garage and got into his Lexus. He sat for a minute trying to figure out where to go. He had plenty of money and could go anywhere. He had mixed emotions, relief and anxiety. Starting the car, he hit the remote to open the garage door, backed out and headed back to the city.

Laura sat trembling for several minutes. Rage flowed through her like a white water river. Finally calming, she got a drink of water from the sink, took several deep breaths and settled down. Looking towards the side door to the garage, she considered it for two or three minutes, then went into the garage and to the metal locker in the corner behind the table saw. It was heavy gauge steel with a lock in the handle. She inspected it for a minute then looked around for something to open it. Finding a screw-driver, she took it to the lock and tried to stick it into the keyway to turn the handle. No go. Stepping back, she stared at the cabinet then looked for something more sub-stantial. She found a claw hammer and a crow bar behind the workbench. Taking these to the cabinet, she pried and tugged at its door, finally bending the metal out. She stuck the crow bar in the opening and pulled with all of her might and the door sprung open. In the dark shadow of the inside, she could barely make out the black canvas bag. She pulled it halfway out, reached to the top zipper and pulled it open enough to get her hand in. A shiver swept through her as she immediately realized what she was touching. She pulled out a wad of hundreds and stared at it like it was an alien being. She pushed the bag back into the cabinet and closed the door as best she could, pushing the table saw against it. She smiled.

Chapter 29

Dino approached the napping Tessio gingerly, as cautious about waking him as he would be to poke a snake with a stick.

"Boss," he said.

Tessio woke with a start and stared at him with venom. "What the fuck do you want?"

"That PI, Ben Roman, called. He said the phone number came back to nothin'. He said that probably means it's a confidential government number, but no way to tell exactly."

Tessio blinked at him. "Government number? Jesus, we got a snitch in the fuckin' woodpile. Get the guys together. We got to have a little talk with that Horseman."

Hornez got the call the following morning. Dino said there was another party on the *Snow White* and that he had to come. Hurry up and get over to the marina, they're planning to leave by one o'clock. Hornez was filled with sludge-like dread, but knew he couldn't refuse. He pulled into the almost empty parking lot a little after twelve and saw Dino and Big Hands standing at the entrance to the slips. "Shit," he muttered to himself.

They waved to him all smiles as he got out of the car and started walking toward them.

They fell in on either side and walked him down the walkway to the end where the boat sat, stoic and gleaming. Walking up the gangplank, Hornez saw no lounging women and he could feel the menace. Tessio came out of the cabin carrying a glass in his thick fist and said, "Welcome aboard, my friend. Come below and have a drink with me."

As Hornez stepped into the cabin, he felt the engines power up and the boat move slowly away from the dock. "Sit," said Tessio, pouring scotch into a water glass. He handed it to Hornez and sat opposite him. "So, you lost your asshole buddy up in New York," he said, taking a gulp from his own glass.

"Yeah. What the hell happened?"

Tessio eyed him. "I'll tell you what happened. Some fuckin' rat set us up. Six mil, gone." He burped. "But, we'll get it back."

"That's good." Hornez felt the sweat run down his back. Tessio eased his bulk up and peered out the sliding doors. Satisfied they were far enough away, he turned back with cold, empty eyes.

"Yeah, that's good, because I think you're the fuckin' rat. Who the fuck you been callin' up in Boston?"

Hornez tried to control his shaking. He felt his bladder loosen. "What do you mean? Nobody."

Tessio took a step toward him, moving surprisingly fast, and slammed his glass into the side of Hornez's head. The glass shattered and sprayed scotch against the bulkhead. An enormous gash opened on the side of Hornez's head and blood gushed out, running down and covering his shirt.

Dino came in and Tessio turned to him. "Do what you got to do to make this rat open up." Dino walked up to a shaking Hornez and slapped him hard across the face. "Who the fuck did you tell about the deal?" Dino screamed. Hornez stared at him in utter shock.

Tessio reached into a locker and pulled out a bolt cutter. "Hold him," he said to Dino. Dino moved around Hornez, pulled his arms out and held them down on the table. Tessio smiled. "Next question," he said and placed the bolt cutter around Hornez's right index finger. "Who the fuck did you tell?" He slammed the cutter closed and took off the finger in a swift cut. Blood now poured from Hornez's hand as well, soaking his lap and mixing with his urine. He started sobbing.

"Please," he said. "No more."

Tessio held the bolt cutter and looked at Dino. Dino smirked. It was quiet for a minute except for the soft sobbing of Hornez and the deep vibrations of the engines.

"There's a guy in Boston," he gasped. "I tell what's going on from time to time and he gives me some money. I don't know who he is."

"Asshole," Tessio said and quickly snipped off Hornez's middle finger. Blood was now covering the floor in a thick ooze.

"Ok, ok, he's a fed. He said his name is Bob Ward. That's all I know. Please!"

Tessio and Dino looked at one another. "A fed?" Tessio mumbled. Turning back to Hornez, he said, "Did you tell him about the deal?" Hornez's head hung and he was staring at the blood pouring from his body. He nodded slowly. Tessio then slammed the bolt cutter into the side of Hornez's head, knocking him onto the floor. "Get the fuckin' net," he said to Dino. Dino reached into a box and pulled out a heavy fishing net. He threw it over Hornez's head and pulled him to his feet. He led him out to the open stern of the boat. The silver towers of Miami gleamed in the distance like some forbidden city of Oz.

He pulled the netting tight around Hornez's legs and snapped on thick line. Hornez stood trussed up and bleeding profusely. Big Hands started hosing the blood off the deck. Tessio got close to Hornez's face.

"Is that who ripped us off?" he asked. Hornez, under the net, shook and tried to shake his head, but couldn't move it. He muttered, "I don't know, please."

"Fuckin' rat," Tessio said and nodded to Dino and Big Hands. Together they lifted Hornez like a bag of garbage and heaved him over the side. After thirty feet, the slack in the line ended and they started dragging Hornez behind the boat, bouncing him over the wake and under water. After a minute, Dino got an M15 rifle out and shot at the floundering Hornez several times. Looking around, Tessio said, "Pull him in, weigh him down and sink the son of a bitch. I got to find out who the fuck this Bob Ward is."

Chapter 30

Angie walked up Beacon Street, with a crisp early October breeze floating over the Public Garden. The trees were in the first stages of their annual burst of color and stood vivid in the clear air. She hardly noticed, thinking about Hughes and why he was so evasive and remote. Her last three calls went to his voice mail with no return call. It was like he changed in the past four weeks. The pedestrian traffic was busy, with a gaggle of young, attractive women coming down from their jobs in the State House. A few brushed Angie as they passed, but she was oblivious to them. Turning the corner onto Joy Street, she went into the dark and cavernous lobby and, using her key, let herself in and up the stairs to Hughes's apartment. She stopped at his door and listened for voices inside. Hearing only the television, she knocked and inserted her key. The door swung open and Hughes looked up from the couch where he was lying.

"Hard at work, I see," Angie said, putting on her best smile.

"Hi, Angie. How ya doin'?"

"Better than you, I think," she replied. "What's going on with you?"

"Nothin'. Just tired," he said softly.

"Danny, talk to me. We're close. Tell me what's going on."

He was quiet for a minute. "It doesn't concern you. It's my problem."

She looked hard at him. "Like it or not, buster, your problem is my problem. What the hell is going on?"

He got up and went to the window. Again he was struck by the seemingly trouble free passersby, A couple walked by, each talking on separate phones. The tops of the trees in the Common shone burnished gold and couples were scattered on the grass. The day was clear, but had lost the summer's brilliance. He stood, not replying, with his hands in his pockets. After a minute, Angie walked over and stood silently next to him, waiting.

He took a breath and finally said, "Angie, I got involved in something with Bill Halloran. I really can't talk about it. Maybe I'll figure it out. But not yet." He looked out the window.

Angie waited then said, "How about we go out for a late lunch? Maybe over to the Parish and we can sit outside with some Cappuccinos. What do you say?"

"Thanks, Angie, but I've got some work to do. At least you got me off my dead ass. I've been working on a locate in East Boston and I have to go over there and look at mailboxes. How about a rain check?"

"Ok, buster. But you know you've got someone to talk to when you're ready."

"You're the best, babe." He kissed her lightly on the cheek and turned away again.

Angie touched him on the arm as she walked past him out of the apartment and closed the door behind her.

Hughes stared out the window for another five minutes, then went to the closet and looked at the zipped and untouched bag. He then called Halloran. The call was answered on the first ring.

"Bill," Hughes started, "I can't live with this. Worse, you're not talking to me and I don't know what's happening. Let's re-think this whole thing."

"Hey, partner. Not good to chat like this. Let's meet at the usual place. I can be there in an hour." Halloran said, then hung up. Hughes threw on a windbreaker and headed for O'Malley's.

The bar was empty, except for the usual day man, Jack, who was wiping glasses behind the bar. Hughes sat and ordered a Dewar's on the rocks. Jack poured it with professional competence and placed it down without a word, but with a smile. Hughes was working on his second scotch when Halloran barged in. He paused, looked around and pointed to a table in the corner. Hughes took his scotch and sat down at it with him. Halloran grinned. "How we doin', partner, good?" He signaled to Jack and asked for a double McCallan's neat. When it arrived, he drank half down.

Hughes also took a deep sip from his glass. "Not so good, Bill. I can't sleep. I'm scared shitless and I can't believe what you got me into."

"You're complaining that you're a rich man? Come on. There's no sweat."

"I don't want the money. I haven't touched it." He paused and took in Halloran's expensive looking suit and enormous Rolex and said, "Apparently not like you."

Halloran's mood changed. "I'm not going to break up our partnership. But, listen, I need you to get a grip and pay attention. There's a little snag. I haven't heard from my CI in a while, then I got a call on my bat-phone. Nothing said, but when I traced the number back, it came from a throwaway cell phone in the south Florida area. I think my guy might be compromised."

"What?" Hughes whispered. "Are you telling me we're made?"

"Nah,nothing like that. But keep your wits about you. Let me know if you see anything out of the ordinary. My CI number goes back to no one. It's untraceable."

"Jesus," Hughes said, staring at Halloran's shirt and tie. "The way you're spending, you stand out like a wart on a tit. I thought we were going to lay low."

"Christ, Danny, I've got to live. Laura and I have got some problems and I moved out. I had to get some clothes."

"Yeah, and a fucking Lexus, " Hughes muttered. "If you've moved out, where's the money?"

"I've got it locked up there. As soon as that bitch is away, I'll get it. Not to worry. How about you?"

"I haven't touched it and I won't. It's dirty, in more ways than one. You can take it."

"Relax, partner. As soon as you settle down, you will realize how lucky you are."

Hughes stared at his glass, then back at Halloran. "The whole thing sucks, especially what you did. If I had any idea, I wouldn't have got involved in any way. I'll watch my ass and somehow hope I can live with myself." He got up and left, leaving Halloran to pay the bill.

Chapter 31

Teddy Constantine's office was on a pier off of Atlantic Avenue. It was inconspicuous among two law firms and an entrance to expensive condos. The sign on the door read Andrews Sales. The door was locked, but there was an intercom with a doorbell affixed on the side. Tessio looked around then pressed the button. After a minute, there was a click and Tessio opened the door and walked into an gritty reception room. There was no one there, and a pile of mail, including *Maxim* and *Penthouse* magazines, sat on the reception counter. The room was paneled with faux walnut wallboard and, aside from the counter, had no furniture. Tessio stood uncertain for a minute then he heard another loud click from the door behind the counter. He opened that and walked into another office. Behind a scarred wooden desk sat Constantine, his feet up on the desk. In the corner sat another man, seriously over weight,, bald and wearing a warm-up suit. Constantine smiled, but didn't get up. The desk was cluttered with scraps of paper, an overflowing ashtray, and some unopened mail. Constantine was wearing a black suit with a white shirt and black tie. He was trim and athletic looking, except for his pale face.

"Hey, Tessio, how you been?" Constantine said as Tessio came in. "Sit."

Tessio dropped his bulk into a captain's chair in front of the desk. "Been better, you?"

"Ok, man. What brings you to Bean Town? Tired of sunshine? Meet Tony," nodding to the man in the corner. Tessio did not bother to look over to him.

"I got a big problem," Tessio said.

"So I hear. Nothin' I can do about that. My part of the deal went down fine."

"We thought it was New York that ripped us off. Almost thought about taking out a guy or two. But then we learned we had a rat." Tessio glanced at the man in the corner who sat motionless. He looked around the room. A window that would have looked out to the boat slips was instead covered with plywood. The walls were bare except for an enlarged photo of a nude woman posing in a garden.

"I never thought New York could pull that off, although there are a couple of asshole cowboys down there," Constantine said.

"The guy we found out was a rat was always hanging around. We should have known better."

"So what's that got to do with me?" Constantine pulled out a cigar and lit it carefully.

"This guy, who no longer is with us, had a phone number that came back to Boston. My shamus tells me it's probably a Fed. I figure the guy was a snitch for the Bureau."

"Constantine looked over to the thug in the corner and smiled. He turned back to Tessio and the smile was gone. "We did the deal as we agreed and your guys got paid. I compliment you on the quality of the product and it is on the street as we talk. But, after we paid our share, I really don't give a fuck what happened to the money. That's your problem."

The two men stared at each other for a minute. Then Tessio said, "We can continue to provide you with good quality stuff and we can consider you a special customer, if you can do a favor."

"What kind of favor?"

"I understand you have a somewhat special relationship with the Bureau here. Perhaps you can inquire if any of their people look like they are spending our money," Tessio talked in a low, moderate tone.

"Constantine eyed him warily. "What do you mean by special relationship? It may be true I have a comfortable working relationship with some people, but we always understand discretion."

"Look," Tessio said. "We don't care who you are friends with as long as you do not know us. But, perhaps you could let me know, just between you and me, if anything stinks over there."

Constantine took a long drag on the cigar and regarded Tessio with cobra eyes. He was quiet for a minute then said, "Our business is going good here with the merchandise we purchased from you. We may be looking for more. If I happen to hear anything, I possibly may make a call. It would be good if you wrote down a phone number where you personally can be reached." He pushed a steno pad and pen across the desk toward Tessio.

Tessio looked at him briefly then wrote down a number. He said, "We always remember favors. We are honorable." With that he stood up.

Constantine didn't bother to stand, but he stubbed out the cigar and nodded. Tessio stood and eased out of the room. As he went out the front door, he heard another loud click as it closed. Atlantic Avenue was bustling with young yuppies, unaware of the business of Andrews Sales.

Chapter 32

Laura hadn't seen or heard from Bill for six days. The kids were driving her crazy and she wondered where he was, but was still happy he was gone. She did hear some noise from the garage late at night a couple of days ago, but when she padded downstairs to check, saw no one. The canvas bag still sat in the garage cabinet, apparently undisturbed, but she couldn't tell for sure. It was Friday night and she had nowhere to go. She poured herself a scotch and sat thinking. Danny Hughes came to mind, not for the first time. She couldn't help noticing his package in the jeans he wore at the cookout. She wondered how hot and heavy he was with that bimbo Angie. Laura knew she had to find out what her husband was up to, and how the bag of money ended up in their garage before she could do anything. She figured that if anyone knew, it was Danny Hughes.

Hughes was making coffee on Saturday morning when the call came in. The temperature outside had dropped and a chilly drizzle was coating the streets with a vinyl sheen. Hughes had dropped a few pounds and did not look as formidable as before. He was actually thinking of talking to a priest. He let the phone ring six times before he answered it.

"Hi, Danny, it's Laura Halloran." Her voice was like warm molasses. "How are you?"

"I'm OK, Laura," Hughes said. "I don't know where Bill is."

"Oh, I really don't care about that. But I really need to talk to you. Can you come by this evening? It's important."

"What is it? Can't you tell me on the phone?"

Laura sighed and lowered her voice to almost a whisper, "I don't think it's a good idea to talk on the phone."

Hughes thought about that. Did this have anything to do with the phone call from Halloran's CI in Florida? After a minute, he said, "OK, I guess I can get by. About what time?"

A pumpkin colored sun was sinking in the west when Hughes turned onto Halloran's street. He drove by twice to see if Bill was home, but he couldn't tell. He parked a distance away where he hoped the Miata would not be spotted.

Laura answered the door on the second knock. She was wearing black jeans and a white silk blouse. It was apparent she was not wearing a bra.

"Hi, Danny. Come on in. You look a little tired," she said.

"Thanks, Laura. Yeah, I haven't been sleeping much lately." Danny stepped into the living room that looked more organized than the last time he had seen it. He noticed the family portrait that hung over the fireplace was gone.

"How about a drink? I've got some good scotch here."

"That sounds good," he replied. "Just put some ice in it."

She headed into the kitchen and Danny notice her jeans were pulled tight over a very nice butt. It swung provocatively as she walked. She came back with two drinks and as she bent over to place his drink on the table, Danny caught a glimpse of a pink nipple. They each sipped their drinks in silence.

Finally, Danny said, "How can I help?" He looked at her with sleepy eyes.

Laura smiled. "Bill's been acting like a real a-hole. Not that it's anything really new, but now he's gone over the edge and I'm through with him. In the meantime, I see him sneaking around in the garage and when I go to see what the hell he's doing, I find a bag full of cash in a locked cabinet. I don't how much is in there, but it sure seems like a lot. More than that fat slob could earn on his own. So, before I blow any whistles, I decided to chat with you to find out what's going on."

Shock shot through Hughes's body like an electric charge. He thought, *Blow the whistle? Christ, what a disaster this is turning out to be.* He sat quietly for a minute, then said, "Laura, I can't tell you anything except to stay as far away as you can."

She sipped her drink and looked back at him. After a moment, she stood up and walked to the front window, the drink still in her hand. She looked out at the quiet suburban neighborhood. Finally, she turned and smiled.

"Danny, I don't know if you noticed, but I paid a lot of attention to you at that cookout we had." She absently fiddled with the buttons on her blouse while she talked, finally undoing two of them. Her left breast was clearly visible, firm and pink tipped. She was not as ample as Angie, but Hughes couldn't stop looking at her. He felt his penis stirring. She noticed and smiled.

"Let's stop kidding ourselves," she said, and put her drink down. She slowly opened the zipper in her jeans. She put both hands on her hips and slid the pants down to her ankles. She was wearing a peach colored thong and the outline of a thick pubic pelt was obvious. Danny felt his heart race. It had been weeks since he'd been with Angie and, try as he might, he couldn't stop the rush of lust.

"Laura, Bill's my friend. You're his wife. I can't."

She opened her blouse all the way. Her nipples were large and hard as erasers.

"Bill's not an issue any longer. As soon as I find out how much I can get, we're completely through. I've already got an attorney doing up the papers," she said.

Then she kicked off her jeans, walked over and kneeled in front of him. Looking steadily up into his eyes, she undid his zipper, reached in and pulled out his erection. With a smile, she put him into her mouth and he felt ecstasy flood his body. She pulled at him for a few minutes and he couldn't stop her. Just when he was getting close, she stopped, stood up and pulled her thong off. Her thick bush was champagne colored and glistening. She grasped his hand and pulled him up. She pushed her hips against his and kissed him deeply. Without resisting, he returned the passion, still unzipped and hard. She then turned and led him up the stairs into the master bedroom. As she entered, she let go of his hand, tossed her blouse off and lay on the bed, her legs open.

Hughes stood, his heart beating fast, in furious excitement. Finally, he said, "I can't. Too many mistakes already in my life."

"Come on, Danny. Give it to me then we can talk money."

That comment did it. He zipped up and took a step

backwards. "Laura, I'm sorry, but this is not right. I've got to go."

She glared at him, then jumped up and threw on a silk robe, leaving it open. "OK, I'll wait. You'll find out what you're missing. As soon as I find out what you guys are up to, I'm going to get my share and fuck you in other ways."

"Laura, don't get involved in anything you don't know about. This never happened and I hope you and Bill can work things out. In the meantime, don't get involved."

Without a word, she walked past him and down the stairs, pulling her robe tight and sitting on the couch. There was a little scotch left in her glass, and she picked it up, looked at it and drank it down. Hughes came into the living room and looked at her. Both were flushed, Laura mostly from anger, Hughes from the arousal. Finally, Hughes said, "Laura, I'm sorry. I can't talk about Bill. I have to go."

She glared at him. "He's up to his ass in something, and I'll bet you're in there with him. I haven't touched that money because I don't know if it's dirty. I figure now that it is. I'll decide whether I should blow the whistle on you assholes or take it for myself."

"Whatever you found, Laura, it won't be good for anyone." He paused. "I've got to go."

He then straightened up and went out the front door, looking both ways for any sign of Halloran, or anyone else.

Chapter 33

Tessio was sprawled on the couch, snoring loudly, when his cell phone rang. The television was showing a golf match, and sunlight streamed through the slider. It took several rings before he regained consciousness and realized what was happening. Rolling over, he found the device in his pocket and answered, "Yeah."

There was silence on the other end for a minute, then, "You dead or alive?"

"Who the fuck is this?"

"A friend in Boston. You asked for a favor. I have a favor to give."

Tessio pulled into a sitting position. He shook off the sleep and said, "You OK on this line?"

"Short and sweet. A friend tells me a guy by the name of Bill Halloran is acting like a real asshole and all of a sudden is throwing money around. You owe me." The phone went dead.

Tessio sat and thought for a minute. *Hard to believe but starting to make sense. That fuckin Horseman was a snitch to the feds. Our guys get ripped off and fucked up and we got a fed all of a sudden spending money. We got to figure this out.*

Tessio yelled for Dino, who was sitting on the patio reading a Penthouse magazine. "Get your ass in here."

Dino came stumbling in, "What's up, boss?"

Tessio was more focused than he'd been in weeks. "Rent a car and head up to Boston. Take that new kid with you. What's his name?"

"Vinnie."

"Yeah. Take him with you. Check into a Motel 6 or something and wait for me to get in touch with you. Don't do nothing, just sit there. Don't be obvious."

"You want us to just sit around?' Dino moaned.

"What did I say? Just sit on your ass until I call you. Start tomorrow."

Tessio pulled out his cell phone and scrolled to Roman's number. He hit the send button and waited as it rang on the other end. After five or six rings, a terse voice said, "Roman."

"You know who this is," Tessio said into the phone. "I want information on a guy in Massachusetts named Bill Halloran. All I know is he works for the Bureau. I need address, description, car he drives and who he's fuckin."

"What office?"

"Boston."

The PI knew better than to ask why. "Give me three days or so. Call you on this number?"

"Yeah, and get off your dead ass and get it as fast as you can." He hung up. Then he yelled to Dino to get him another throwaway phone. He lurched over to the wet bar and poured a half glass of McClellan's. "Son of a bitch," he muttered to himself. Then he yelled to Dino to get going to Boston.

Halloran pushed the folder across his desk and looked around the room. Most desks were empty and the agents that were in had their heads down. The usual frat boy camaraderie seemed to have cooled for him lately. *Who cares*, he thought to himself. He reached into his pocket and pulled out a wad of cash. Holding it down below his desk, he counted it out and frowned. *Time to hit the kitty again.* He got up and started toward the door. Bob Hearns, a surveillance squad guy, looked up and said, "Meeting another CI?" Halloran caught the sarcasm in his voice. He shrugged and went downstairs to the parking lot, got in his Lexus and pulled out onto Federal Street.

Despite the chilly weather, Faneuil Hall was bustling with tourists and street performers. He picked up the expressway and headed south. His neighborhood was quiet as he turned onto his street. He parked across from an empty lot and walked up his driveway, looking for any sign of Laura. He could tell she was home because the van was sitting in the driveway. The garage door was open so he could walk in silently. Once inside the garage, he stopped and listened for any noise from inside the house. Hearing nothing, he silently walked to the locker and looked closely at it. The damage Laura did was not obvious and he wondered about it. He took out his key and opened it. The bag sat there. Was it moved? He wasn't sure. He unzipped it and reached inside, pulling out a wad of bills which he quickly stuffed in his jacket pocket. He closed and locked the cabinet and left. He complimented himself on his stealth.

Inside the house, Laura watched from the kitchen window.

Chapter 34

What had been a dry and mostly sunny fall changed abruptly into a dark, gray and rainy November. Streets were swept with running rivets of water and were noticeably emptied of pedestrians. Trees had mostly dropped their leaves and stood like dark skeletons against the pewter sky. Hughes sat at his desk staring at a report he'd just written when he heard the scrape of a key in the door lock and a faint knock.

"Danny?" Angie called as she slowly pushed the door open.

"Yeah, I'm here," he replied, standing to watch her come in. She was wearing snug black jeans, and a white silk blouse under a velvet blazer. Her black hair curled to her shoulders. Hughes felt a familiar stirring but showed indifference.

"What's going on, Danny?" she asked. "You don't call and you don't answer. You all right?"

"Yeah, I'm ok," he replied, sitting back at the desk.

Angie stood silent for a minute, then walked over and sat on the couch, looking at him. "Something's wrong and different. How about remembering who I am and talking to me about it?"

He shrugged, got up and headed to the kitchen. "Nothing to talk about. Coffee?"

"Sure." She was quiet while he fiddled with the coffee maker.

He made the coffee without looking at her, then poured two cups. He brought one to her and carried the other back to his desk. They both took small sips without comment.

"Danny," she said, "we have something special. I think better than most. At least I thought so. I can tell when you're happy and I can tell when you're stressed. I know something is really wrong. Who else can you talk to about it?"

"Nothing really to talk about," he said. He put his coffee cup down and looked into it.

"I've got a feeling it's got something to do with the creepy FBI guy you hang around with. That guy Halloran." she said.

Hughes looked up, startled. He shrugged.

Confirming what she suspected, Angie continued. "That asshole has gotten you into something you don't like, hasn't he? He's a sleazy creep and way below you."

"I can't really talk about it," he said, looking back into his coffee cup.

Angie stood and stared at him. "Yes you can and you will. I'm Angie. We shared secrets. We have times in the vault that we will never reveal." She took long strides to him, stood quiet for a minute, then put her arms around him. Hughes let her and felt her hard thighs and soft breasts against him. He dropped his head onto her shoulder. He was silent for a minute, then took a deep breath.

"Angie, we ripped some guys off and it got out of control." His voice was small and ragged.

"Ripped off who? What?"

Hughes stared at her. "A couple of drug mules. It was supposed to be foolproof, but I know, nothing is."

Angie leaned back to look into his eyes. It was silent in the apartment except for a sharp November wind that rattled the windows.

"OK," she said, pulling back. "Got any wine?" She went to the refrigerator and found a half bottle of Chardonnay. Pulling the cork, she sniffed at the top of the bottle and nodded her head. She took two glasses from the cupboard, poured the wine and brought them to the couch.

"Time to tell me about it," she said, handing him one of the glasses.

Hughes was silent, but picked up the wine glass and took a deep sip. He looked into Angie's eyes and shrugged.

"OK, Bill had a CI in Miami. An inside guy in the mob down there. He told Bill about a major drug deal going down. Apparently, the Miami guys did a major score with Columbians and were going to sell serious quantity to New York and Boston guys."

Angie drained her glass and got up for the bottle, which she brought over and refilled the two glasses. "What kind of drugs?" she asked.

"Coke, and a lot of it. Bill's idea was to let the deal go through, then hit the couriers for the cash. He said they obviously couldn't call law enforcement and Bill said he could make it look like either New York or Boston did a double cross. He said it was foolproof."

"How much money?"

"Lots. Maybe five to six plus mil in total."

"Jesus. You actually did this?"

"Yeah, and it's been eating at me ever since. It's beginning to look less and less foolproof." Hughes sighed and stared out the window at the gathering dark clouds.

Angie stared at him. "Do you have some of the money?"

"Yeah."

"How much?"

"I don't know exactly, maybe a couple, three mil."

"Jesus Christ."

"Yeah."

Angie stared at him in disbelief. "Where is it now?" she asked.

"It's in the closet. I haven't touched it. But that's not the worst part. Bill blew one of the couriers away during the heist. I think he planned to do it all along to help cover us. I couldn't believe it."

"Are you serious?" she whispered. "He killed someone? Did you know?"

"I'm sick over this. I've followed the papers. There's all kinds of speculation as to what happened. Apparently the other guy refuses to talk. They are even considering it a gay bashing thing. But I can't get it out of my head. I can't sleep. I'm sick." Hughes got up and walked to the window that was now streaked with rain.

"Danny, you got sucked into something you wanted no part of. Give the damn money back and stay away from Halloran," Angie said.

"Give it back to who? And, no matter how you look at it, I'm an accessory." Hughes stepped back from the window, pale.

"You never gave a shit about money, " she said. "We were having a good and full life, without a lot of stuff. Somehow we have to get back to where we were."

Hughes shrugged and stood silent. Angie looked at

him with a combination of love, pity, and disgust. She drained her wine, stood and walked to the door.

"Try to sort this out. I'll help however I can, but right now I have no idea how this can be resolved. I'm going to think about it and you." With that she left, closing the door softly behind her. Hughes thought for a minute then went to the closet, opened the door and stared at the black duffel, squashed into a corner like a crouching predator. After a minute, he went back to the window and caught a glimpse of Angie as she turned the corner from Joy Street onto Beacon. Somehow, he felt better.

Chapter 35

Dino was lying on the bed watching a porn movie when his cell phone rang. Vinnie looked up from the tabloid he was reading and waited for Dino to answer. Dino fished the small phone from his pocket and pushed the answer button.

"Yeah."

"Yeah, your ass," Tessio hissed on the other end of the call. "Wake up and try to have some smarts."

Dino sat up at attention. "What's up, boss?" he asked.

"Something stinks about this guy up there. The guy Halloran. I think the stink may be coming from our money. I need you to start looking around."

"What do you want us to do?"

"I got a package from my gumshoe. It's got information about this asshole in it. I'm going to send it to you. Then do a drive-by at his house and take a look. Don't let anyone see you and don't act suspicious. Got that? I'll tell you when to do anything else."

Moans and groans were coming from the television. Dino yelled, "Vinnie, turn that down." Then, into the phone, "OK, boss. Got it. We're on it."

Tessio clicked the phone off then made another call immediately. It was answered on the fifth ring. "Yeah."

Tessio smiled to himself. "Constantine."

"No, who the fuck is this?"

"Constantine. It's your fat Miami friend."

The laugh reverberated across the lines. "Tessio, you fat fuck. What can I do to or for you?"

"You know, my friend, we suffered a great loss."

Constantine chuckled. "I heard." Then his voice got hard, "I also heard Miami boys were talking up that we were suspected. We are honorable up here and do not appreciate being falsely accused."

"Constantine, we know your people are standup. We never thought your people could be involved," Tessio said.

Constantine softened. "We are brothers. What can we do for you?"

"May we meet the day after tomorrow? I have something to discuss with you."

"My door is always open. Come to Giacamo's on Salem Street the day after tomorrow at three o'clock. I'll make sure the pasta is fresh and the place quiet. I look forward to seeing you." Constantine hung up quickly, aware of the necessity of short phone calls.

Tessio flew up two days later with Rocco, his cousin. He waddled out to a waiting black Buick that sat at the arrivals curb being purposely overlooked by the state police charged with keeping traffic moving. Tessio shivered in the late November air as he got in, and the car plowed past the steady stream of travelers. Heavy clouds hung over the city as they rode the short distance from the airport to the Sumner tunnel. Exiting the tunnel, the heavy car swung around and into the congestion of the North End. Salem Street was sandwiched between aging brownstones and a jumble of restaurants and tiny shops. The car, with Tessio and Rocco staring out the windows in back, made its way slowly up the street, finally stopping in front of a small bistro with an ornate oak and glass door. There was a menu to the side of the entrance featuring a variety of veal dishes and homemade pastas. Tessio heaved himself out of the car, followed by Rocco, and told the driver to return in an hour. The driver, a large head sitting on massive shoulders with no apparent neck, remained looking straight ahead and nodded. The car pulled away slowly, nudging pedestrians out of its way. Rocco tried the door and found it locked. It was ten minutes after three and a cold rain was threatening. Tessio looked up and down the street in acute awareness.

Within seconds, a man almost as fat as Tessio unlocked the door from within. As Tessio and Rocco entered, Constantine, dressed in a shiny, shark-gray suit, high collared white shirt and gray silk tie, bellowed from a table in the corner. "Come in, my friends from the south. Come in."

The restaurant of eight tables was empty of patrons. Tessio could see two young waiters, wearing white shirts and black pants, standing at attention next to the open kitchen. The sweet smell of fresh tomato sauce and grilled meat wafted through the air. The warmth of the restaurant was inviting after the chill of the outside.

Constantine and a companion stood up and waved to Tessio and Rocco. The fat man had disappeared, but Tessio knew he was nearby. A plate of crispy fried calamari and red wine magically appeared. Constantine scooped a portion onto his plate and took a sip of the wine, smiling with satisfaction.

"What brings you to our humble home?" he asked.

Tessio grabbed the rest of the calamari and took a deep swig of wine. He started talking with his mouth half full. "You know about our problem?" he said.

"Yes. Way too much money was lost. I must say the product you brought to us is of excellent quality so we were saddened to hear of the outrageous theft you suffered. But, we cannot help with money, if that's what you are here for."

"No, we are big boys and do not come seeking handouts. What I need is another favor of your knowledge and resources of your hometown," said Tessio.

Constantine looked at him closely. "In what way, my friend?"

"We discovered a rat in our bed and traced his calls back to Boston. The Bureau, in fact."

"I assume you have dealt with the rat?" Constantine asked. Steaming plates of pasta arrived, along with side plates of meatballs.

"Yes. And we have a lead to who in the Bureau the rat was reporting. The more we look at that asshole, the more he looks like the scumbag that ripped us off."

Constantine shrugged. "You think?" he said. "I understand one of your people got clipped during the rip. Employees of the government generally do not do anything like that."

"All I know is this guy all of a sudden is spending a lot of money and acting like a big shot. We know it was none of your people and now I don't even believe any of the cowboys in New York would have the cajones to pull off the job. So this FBI asshole looks more and more like it."

"So, how can I help?"

Tessio looked around. The two waiters stood at a distance and the chef was bending over a steaming kettle in the kitchen. The front door was locked and only the four men occupied the dining area. He smiled and spooned a portion of pasta onto his plate, swirling some onto his fork and sucking it into his mouth. "I have two men here, but they are weak and stupid. Not enough to watch this guy and maybe figure out if he's the one and maybe see who the other guy is. If he's the guy, we need to find our money and get it back. If he is not reasonable, I will need cover with the agency. I hear you may have some influence with the U.S. attorney."

Constantine was quiet for several minutes. "It is true we have friends. And I have a crew. Perhaps we can do this favor."

"Favors are never forgotten," Tessio whispered. The four men ate and drank and talked of the stupidity of law enforcement and the price of women. On the way back to the airport, Tessio called Dino and told him to quietly determine the daily schedule of Special Agent Halloran and his family.

Chapter 36

Hughes felt a little better after Angie's visit. He stripped off the sweatpants he'd been wearing for days and stepped into the shower. Halfway through, he heard the phone ringing. Swearing softly, he walked dripping naked to the phone, picked it up and listened.

"Danny, it's me." He heard Halloran's voice, excited and shrill. "You dead or alive?"

"I'm here. What do you want?" Hughes shivered and looked for something to throw over his shoulders.

"Meet me. Usual place. Two o'clock."

Hughes thought for a minute. He wanted nothing to do with Halloran, but had to know what was going on. "OK. See you there." He heard a loud click as Halloran hung up without another word.

The rain had washed the streets clean and the thin light of late fall gave a fresh look to the usual gloom of the season. The air was damp as Hughes made his way to O'Malley's. He was wearing his Red Sox jacket and ball cap and fit into the bar's clientele like coffee with the donut. Halloran was seated at the usual rear booth. His face was red and blotchy and his hair was longer. Hughes walked over to him, with only a brief nod from Jack, who was working the bar. Only one couple sat at the bar, paying no attention to anyone but themselves. Hughes glanced at them and the private investigator in him immediately recognized an affair. Halloran gave a lizard like smile and raised his glass in a solemn toast as Hughes sat down.

"Hey, Danny," he said, draining the last of his scotch and signaling to the bartender for two more.

"Bill." Danny saw his eyes were marbled with red. He thought back just weeks ago when both he and Halloran were joking and being silly. "What's going on?"

"Thought we'd get caught up. You got your stash secured?"

Hughes glanced around. "I haven't touched it. In fact I want to return it."

"What the fuck are you talking about? Return it to who? It didn't belong to anyone in the first place. All dirty money. We are the washers."

"Bill, I can't sleep. I never thought you would do what you did. It's made me sick."

"Look," Halloran replied in a whisper, "what happened was necessary. No one has any idea about us."

"You sure about that? I keep thinking all the shit in the world is going to drop on me."

Halloran looked around again at the near empty bar. The bartender was laughing into a cell phone and the couple was getting hot and heavy. "You see anyone lurking around?"

"What do you mean, lurking?"

"You know, seeing the same person twice or more."

"Are you saying you're being followed?" Hughes's voice elevated and Halloran gestured with his hand to keep it low.

"Not that, exactly. But I noticed the same car drive by the house a couple of times, so I ran its plate. Came back to a rental. Who the fuck rents cars in Pembroke?"

"Jesus, Bill," Hughes said. "You've been acting like a lottery winner. You think no one notices that watch? The car?" He gestured out the window where the Lexus sat in front of a fire hydrant.

"I got to live," Halloran mumbled. "I think maybe that bitch I'm married to suspects something and may have said something."

Hughes had a momentary flash of Laura's naked body, then pushed it quickly out of his mind. "What can she suspect, except that you're spending money like you're in congress, drinking like a fish and smelling like a New Orleans whore house."

"I think she's too stupid to really figure out anything. I only go to the house to get some walking around money. We've been on the outs for some time, I just made it halfway official. I moved out, but I send over money every week for the kids."

Hughes was silent as the bartender brought over two glasses filled to the brim with scotch. He waited until he saw him return to the bar and pick up his cell phone again.

"Bill, I can't take it," Hughes said again. "I couldn't keep it inside and I talked to Angie."

Halloran looked at him with eyes as big as marbles. "You did what?"

"I talked to Angie. She said I should give the money back and get as far away from it as possible."

Halloran grew red. The anger came off him like a decaying stink. "You think because I spend a little of it I'm going to fuck it up, and you go and blab your mouth off."

Halloran chugged down his scotch and held his glass up for the bartender.

Quietly, Hughes said, "I can't forget that night and what you did, that I'm a part of it."

"Grow up, my friend. You want something, you've got to take it, regardless. I've spent years in the Bureau watching scumbag guys take what they want and live the good life."

Hughes took a small sip of his scotch and looked down into the amber liquid. After a minute, he said, "Look, Bill, I will do anything I can to get out of this. But why did you ask me to come here? No offense, but I would rather stay away."

"I'm wondering if you've seen anything suspicious," Halloran said, calming down.

"What do you mean suspicious?" Hughes asked warily.

"I don't know. I just got a bad feeling. Maybe I'm paranoid. I don't trust that bitch Laura. Seems like some of the guys in the office are looking at me weird."

"Look, Bill. I haven't done shit since the rip-off. I've been hunkering down in my apartment, trying to figure out what to do. I don't want any of the money and wish to God I never got involved with you. I haven't noticed anything, but I'll keep my eyes open. If someone is onto us, I don't know what to do," Hughes said softly.

Halloran downed his drink and again held his glass up for the bartender. He smiled at Hughes. "Don't sweat it, Danny. I'll take care of anything that happens."

Hughes pushed his glass to the middle of the table. He got up and shook his head slowly. He walked out of the bar without another word, wondering how his life had collapsed so fast.

Chapter 37

A ngie was scheduled for a double, but after the first shift she managed to talk her co-worker Melissa into taking the second. The pit in her stomach was matched only by her resolve. She called Dan.

"Hey. How are you feeling?" she asked after he answered on the fourth ring.

"I'm OK. I just wish I could figure a way out," he said, softly. "It looks like I'm screwed whichever way I go."

"We've got to figure a way to get it all back," she said. The depression in his voice scared her. Danny Hughes was always the tough guy. He never backed down from confrontation, but now he seemed vulnerable.

"I wish I could," he said. "If I go to the cops, I'm involved that way. If I go to the bad guys, they will know who I am and will figure out who Bill is in no time. It's the proverbial rock and a hard place."

"You owe nothing to Halloran. He got you into this. Think about yourself."

"I know, Angie. Problem is, I've been sucked into a very ugly situation with no way out. I keep thinking I could just take the money and run, but somehow it doesn't seem right. I wouldn't even think to ask you to go with me."

Angie was silent as she thought about that. Then she said, "Danny, you've got too much going for you in many different ways. I can't see you running away and being able to sleep soundly. I'm with you, but I don't think that's a good option."

"Yeah. It's tainted money. And, somehow I know it's going to hit the fan. Bill thinks he hit a homerun, but I think he's hit into a double play."

"I don't know what to do. All I know is this is not a good spot to be in and somehow you have got to get out. Get the money back without them knowing about you." Angie said after a little hesitation. "I want to go back to the way we were. I loved you better then."

Hughes nodded to himself. "OK, Angie. I'll try to figure this out. But, we agree, running is not an option."

"I love you, Danny."

"I love you, too."

Angie sat and thought for a while. She figured the only way it could end is if the money was given back and if no one went looking for whoever killed the guy, either the cops or the mob. She didn't even know to whom the money could be returned. And, keeping Danny out of a murder investigation was critical. After all, he really had nothing to do with it. The more she thought about it, the more she figured Bill Halloran was the key to both. Dan had told her Halloran was going over the edge, leaving his wife and kids, spending money and living like a drunken teenager. Halloran actually scared her a little. He never said exactly what he did with the Bureau and he never seemed to be without a gun. She wondered how much Laura knew about what was going on. With feminine resolve, she decided it was time to talk to her.

Chapter 38

The phone call to Laura was awkward. Angie could tell she was wary of her and while she consciously wondered why, she instinctively knew there was female competition there. The traffic out of Boston and down to the South Shore was thick and chaotic. Angie piloted her Mustang expertly, but it still took almost an hour to arrive. She parked in front and noticed only the Prius was in the driveway. The street seemed quiet and empty.

Laura answered the door dressed in jeans and a baggy sweatshirt. Her makeup looked fresh, but her face was drawn and tight. She gave Angie a half smile.

"Hi, Laura," Angie said as she walked into the pristine living room. "How are the kids?"

"Kids are OK. Not so sure about myself. Would you like a glass of wine?"

"Wine would be good."

"Chardonnay OK? I've got some in the fridge." Laura turned toward the kitchen, her high heels clicking on the wood floor.

Angie sat on a couch that looked brand new and looked around the room. On the mantle were three photos in silver frames of the Halloran family. One photo was taken at what appeared to be a ski resort, white icing covered the mountains in the background. Laura and the kids were beaming with health, but Bill looked pained. Laura came back in a minute, carrying two stem glasses filled almost to the brim with golden wine. She sat across from Angie and tried another weak smile. Each of the women took sips from the wine and sat quietly.

Angie started. "Laura, I think we both are pulled into something terribly bad. How much do you know about what is going on?"

Laura took a deep drink from her glass and sighed. "I know somehow Bill got ahold of a huge bag of cash and has become a total asshole. Our marriage is over and I can't wait to move past him. And some strange character came looking for him."

"Do you know what happened when they got the money?" Angie asked tentatively.

"I don't even know where he got it."

Angie waited, then, "It's worse than you can imagine. Apparently Bill got this idea of ripping off a drug deal in New York. They got away with a lot of money, but Bill killed a guy during the robbery. Danny had no idea Bill was going to do that and he got pulled in, stupidly."

Laura sat in shock. "Killed a guy? What? Killed who?"

"Apparently one of the criminal drug guys. Danny said the cops think it was a rival gang rip-off, but he's not so sure people aren't looking more closely at it. Not to mention the guys that owned the money."

"Jesus. You mean that asshole is involved in murder?

"It doesn't seem to bother Bill, but it's killing Danny. I can't see a way out." Angie drained her wine and held the glass out for Laura to refill.

Laura nodded and went back to the kitchen, returning

with a bottle of white and refilled both glasses. Her face was pale. "It gets better," she said. "Two goons showed up here yesterday. It was like badgers were standing at the front door. They leered at me like I had no clothes on and said they were looking for Bill. These guys were not cops. They were something a lot worse."

Angie took another sip and thought for a minute. "I wish I knew how to help. It's like a horror movie. You can't go to the cops and you don't even know who you are dealing with on the other side."

"I can't stand it," Laura said. "I'm going to call Bill and confront him. He doesn't know that I hid the money."

"OK, I'm getting out of here. If anything breaks, please let me know. Danny's bag of money is still in his closet, untouched. It's like living with a snake." Angie drained her wine and put it down on the coffee table. She stood and crossed her arms. "Good luck to us."

Laura looked at her for a minute, then walked over and put her arms around her. The two women hugged for an instant, knowing their lives would never be the same again. Angie walked out, got into her car and sat thinking. Nothing really seemed to be accomplished, but somehow she felt better. She backed out and slowly made her way up the street, past the perfect houses and well tended lawns, never noticing the two men slumped down in the innocuous sedan as she drove by.

"Who the fuck was that?" Vinnie asked Dino, as Angie disappeared around the corner.

"How am I supposed to know," Dino replied, looking at his cell phone. "Probably girl on girl action. You know how these housewife broads are. I just got a message from Tessio. He wants us to have a little talk with the FBI asshole. He must be pretty sure he's our guy." Vinnie shrugged and slid down in his seat to wait some more.

Inside, Laura punched in the number to Halloran's regular cell phone. He was pulling on his jacket and leaving his office as the call came in. Outside, tourists were crowded in Faneuil Hall, watching street entertainers and eating junk food. Life in the city pulsed.

Seeing the call was from Laura, he answered with a curt, "What."

"Angie was here. I know what you did, " Laura said over the phone.

Halloran stopped in his tracks. His face was a blank page. "What are you talking about?" he asked.

"I put that money you stole away so you can't hurt anyone else. I think maybe we should talk."

Halloran was stunned. "You put what money away?" he asked, afraid of the answer.

"If you're not here in an hour, I'm burning it."

"Fuck you. Don't do shit until I get there. You have no idea what you are dealing with," he said, punching the call off.

Dino and Vinnie watched the government sedan lurch around the corner and pull into the driveway. They smiled. Halloran immediately went into the garage and opened the cabinet. "Son of a bitch," he muttered and went into the house. He found Laura sitting at the kitchen table, a glass of wine and a legal pad in front of her.

"What did you do with it?" he yelled. Laura smiled at him.

She sat with the half smile for a minute then said, "Tell me the whole ugly thing. Are you a murderer as well as a philanderer and asshole?"

"Where's my money?" Halloran hissed. The rage was building and his face was turning red.

"Where you can't find it," she said. "That money will destroy you and us in the process. I don't care how you are going to do it, but you need to give it back. You know, two guys showed up here looking for you?"

"What two guys? What are you talking about?"

"You think you're so clever, but obviously they are on to you. Two goons are looking for you. They're not handing out Scientology leaflets."

Halloran stared at her in disbelief. How could anyone know?

A quarter of a mile away, Dino and Vinnie watched the house, unaware of what was going on inside.

"That's our boy," Dino said and Vinnie nodded. "Let's give him some more time and then have a little talk with him." Vinnie smiled and scratched his belly.

Inside the house, Halloran was staring at his wife in uncontrolled anger. "Where the fuck is my money," he hissed.

Laura turned her back to him and said, "The kids will be here soon. You sure you want to do this?"

Halloran raised his fist to her then put it back down. He fought to control himself at the mention of his children. "OK, Laura, you have no idea what you are doing. Let's cut out the bullshit and get this finished. First, where's the money?" he said with a shred of control.

"I'm not telling you anything until you tell me what you did and what's going to happen."

"Look, I pulled off a perfect job. Even if we are on the outs, there is enough to keep you and the kids happy for the rest of your lives. We were done a long time ago, we just didn't know it. Get realistic here and let me get the money and get out of here. I have to figure out who came by." Halloran was trying his best to gain control.

Then they heard a knock on the door. Both Halloran and Laura turned and looked at the front hall, perplexed.

"You expecting someone?" Halloran asked her.

"No." She walked to the front window and peered outside, but couldn't see anyone.

"Answer it," he whispered. "I'll stay behind the door just in case. If it's just a nobody, get rid of them."

Laura went to the door while Halloran stood behind it. She opened it and gasped as she saw the same two men from before. She took an involuntary step back.

"We need to speak to him," Dino hissed. Laura stepped back some more and looked over to where Halloran stood. Dino caught the glance and pushed the door all the way open, exposing Halloran. He stepped in front of the two men.

"What the fuck do you guys want," he said, looking both straight in the eyes. He pushed his jacket aside to show his Glock. "I'm a federal agent. Get the hell away from my house."

Dino smiled. "There is someone in Miami that wants to talk with you. Feel like taking a trip?"

"I'm not going anywhere. Get the fuck away from here."

Dino looked at Vinnie, who shrugged. "Well, if you won't go there, he'll come here. That will be more difficult for everyone."

Halloran glanced behind him to Laura, who was ashen white. He knew what was being implied. He looked back at the two men and then looked up and down the street. He saw no one else and figured nothing was going to happen right then. He put his hand on his gun butt and said,

"Get out of here. If someone wants to talk to me, they can make an appointment at the FBI office." With that, he stepped back and slammed the door. Dino and Vinnie turned laughing, and headed up the road to where the rental car was parked. Dino decided he would tell Tessio that he was right, this FBI asshole was the guy and something had to be done.

Chapter 39

Halloran was shaken. He could not understand exactly how they found out, unless his CI in Florida gave him up. He had not heard from him in a couple of months. He looked at Laura, who stared at him with horror in her eyes. She turned and stomped into the kitchen. After a minute, Halloran followed. "OK, where the fuck is the money? If I don't have it, I'll have nothing to bargain with."

She stared at him with growing hatred, unsure of what to do. Finally she walked to the kitchen window that looked out to the back yard. "I buried it," she said. "It's out by the fence. Stick it where the sun doesn't shine."

"Bitch," he said and stormed out of the house, striding to the rear of the yard. He could clearly see where she had buried the bag, and he headed into the garage for a shovel. Minutes later, he dug the bag out, brushed it off and carried it out to his car. He tossed it into the back and covered it with a tarp. Far down the road, using powerful binoculars, Dino watched him. He quickly speed-dialed Tessio and said, "He's got one of the bags, all we have to do is figure out where the other one is and take them back, one way or another."

Halloran jumped into his car and sped off, turning the

corner and failing to notice the two Miami men, parked a ways up the street. He headed toward Boston flushed with anger and with no destination in mind. When he hit the expressway north, traffic had come to a dead stop because of an accident. It gave him some time to cool down. Thinking a little more clearly, he telephoned Hughes, who answered on the third ring.

"Where are you?" Halloran asked.

"I'm driving to Wakefield. I've got a case," Hughes yelled into his phone over the road noise.

"Turn around and meet me at O'Malley's. We got a problem."

The after-work crowd was drifting in and there was an undercurrent of noise, like a distant beehive. Halloran parked in front of a hydrant outside and walked in, stopping to let his eyes adjust. Hughes was not there yet. Halloran went to the bar, pushed in between two suits and nodded to Jack. The bartender ambled his buffed bulk down to him and gave a weak smile. "Double Black Label, neat," Halloran said. Jack's smile widened and he half filled a rocks glass and pushed it to Halloran, who swigged it down, and nodded for another. Bret shrugged and refilled the glass from the bottle, smiled again, and shuffled down to two blondes who were looking for a refill. Hughes came in ten minutes later, looked around and found Halloran still at the bar. He joined him.

"Parking was a bitch. What's up?" Hughes looked and sounded tired.

"Let's go outside. Can't talk here," Halloran said. He downed the rest of his drink, tossed a fifty on the bar and headed to the front door. Hughes trailed behind, weaving around the crowd that had gotten thick. Outside, Halloran started walking toward State Street, ignoring the bustle. Hughes fell in beside him. "What's up?" he asked again.

"A couple of scumbags came to the house. Somehow they figured out we were involved. Not only that, that bitch Laura found the money and tried to hide it from me. She threatened to blow a whistle, although she doesn't know who to blow it to."

Hughes turned white as they passed Faneuil Hall and continued toward the Garden.

"How the hell did they find out?" he asked.

"I think they made my CI and somehow put two and two together. They want a meeting, apparently with a heavy."

"What are you going to do?" Hughes asked.

"I got to find out what they know. And, I've got to find out who the fuck they are. I need you for back-up."

Hughes slowed to a shuffle. "Bill, I've got to tell you, all bets are off since you pulled the trigger. I've been talking with Angie and all I want is out. Take the money."

"You can't bail now, buddy boy. I need you to cover my ass." Halloran's voice turned hard as stone.

An icy wind funneled in from the harbor, kicking up dust and trash. Heads were turned down as the commuters pushed against it and hurried along. Hughes glanced over to Halloran and felt nauseous. ughes glqnce

"Are you fuckin' nuts? Put the money in a locker and mail the key to them and get away from this whole thing. My share goes in there with yours. I want out."

"Not that easy. If they figured us for the money, they figured us for blowing away their courier. I don't want to get into an eye for an eye deal."

Dusk was moving in. Hughes stopped next to an entrance to a pub that was filling up with after work patrons. With a shiver, he looked at Halloran and saw him clearly in the street lights. Hughes realized how trivial the idea of fast money was in comparison to what he really wanted. He had the love of a fabulous woman who was standing by him, regardless of his stupidity and mistakes. He could earn a living and had the respect of his clients. He saw his future hanging precariously. He suddenly knew what he should do.

"Bill, you sucked me into a horrible situation. You committed a despicable act to cover another despicable act. Now I want out. I haven't touched the money and I won't. I will give it back and hope I have some life to save. I will not help you with anything beyond that." His voice for the first time in weeks was firm with resolve.

Halloran looked up and down the street for a minute. "You pussy," he said harshly. "OK, I'll give your money back, but if you rat me out, I'll fuckin' kill you too." In his head, he was already considering how he could set Hughes up for the heist and killing.

Chapter 40

Halloran turned and walked away, leaving Hughes standing alone in the crowd of people. After a minute, he headed back to his Miata, parked several blocks away near Faneuil Hall. He was alone in his thoughts as he walked. The duffel bag of money was still in his closet untouched. He wanted desperately to get rid of it, but had no idea how or to whom he could return it. He still needed Halloran if he had any chance of getting out of this nightmare. He thought about running, but quickly dismissed that. As far as he knew, the mob had not linked him with Halloran. If the money could be returned anonymously, maybe they would quit trying. Still, he was an accessory to murder. If the mob wanted revenge, they would start with Halloran and continue from there. He had no idea how they fingered Halloran. So much for a "perfect" plan.

And the mob was only half of the problem. Criminal prosecution was still a possibility.

The small sports car was parked where he had left it, poised and silent, with a bright orange parking ticket stuck on the windshield. Hughes shrugged, got in and started the car, the exhaust giving a satisfying blast. Shifting into first, he slowly pulled out and drove the short distance to

Joy Street, parking at a meter on Beacon Street. The early darkness had moved in and the antique streetlights were making soft pools of orange light in the Common. Still lost in thought, he climbed the stairs, unlocked the door to his apartment and went in. He stopped cold, surprised to see Angie sitting at the window, her bare feet up on the sill, a cup of coffee in her hand.

She didn't turn to look at him, but said, "Welcome home, buster. Missed ya." She was wearing tight blue jeans and a starched white shirt. She looked like she'd been relaxing for some time. Hughes shuffled in a few feet, stopped, looked at her and for the first time in weeks, smiled.

"Jesus, Angie, am I glad to see you. It's like walking out of a shit storm." Hughes said. She smiled back, stood up, and stretched.

"I thought you could use a little cheering up," she said, bringing her coffee cup to the small kitchenette and rinsing it. "What some coffee? There's some left but it's not too fresh."

"That would be good." He sat down heavily on one of the two chairs at the small table. She placed the coffee down in front of him and sat opposite. He looked up gratefully as she placed the coffee down and sat opposite.

Hughes took a sip and looked into Angie's eyes. "They're on to us. To Bill, at least. So it's only a matter of time until I'm fingered as well."

"Who?" Angie asked.

"I guess it's the Miami mob. They're the ones that lost the money. Somehow, they tracked it back to Bill. He thinks his informant down there may have said something, but he hasn't heard from the guy in quite a while. I told him I just want to give everything back and pretend it never happened."

"What did Bill say?"

"He wants to play hard ball. I think he's gone nuts."

Angie was quiet for a moment, then got up and poured the rest of the coffee into her mug. She sat back down and said, "I went down to talk to Laura. Their marriage is destroyed and she just wants to get away from him. So, you're right. He's gone over the edge."

Hughes was stunned. "You talked to her about this? What does she know about it?"

"Not much, but she found the money. She was going to hide it from him and use it as a bargaining chip. I gather they don't talk to each other anymore, so she doesn't know any of the details or where it came from."

Hughes sipped his coffee in anguished thought. "Angie, I don't know what to do. It keeps closing in on me. I'm feeling completely trapped." He was quiet for a minute, then said softly, "And I'm scared."

"Danny, you're my white knight. I've never known you to be scared of anything. You have to pull up the inner strength I know is there. It's easy to think about fast money and to fantasize about a new life it can bring. That's hollow, and in the long run, worthless. But what you have inside, what you are made of is what's real and important. You made a mistake. You had nothing to do with the way it got out of control, but it's up to you to make it somehow right for you, and me. She got up and walked to the window.

"If you work at it, I know you will do what's right. No matter where that money came from or where it was going, it does not belong to you. Get it back to where it belongs. And Bill Halloran is not your friend. He used you and you owe him nothing. Let's figure out how to do what's right, even if it hurts. You can only be true to yourself by pulling up the character I know is in there and that I love about you. We can work this out and take the punishment, whatever it is. Punishment is better than living in fear or running. Life really comes down to a few simple things: love, integrity, and honesty. We can have that if we want it."

Hughes looked at her. His face had slackened and paled. After a minute, he whispered, "You're right. Thank you. I'll do what I have to do."

She gave back a small smile. "OK," she said, standing and taking his hand. "Let's go to bed and see how close we can get."

Chapter 41

Halloran was sitting at the bar in O'Malley's. Jack was working, polishing glasses and glancing at Halloran from time to time out of the corner of his eye. Three double Johnnie Walker Blacks had already been drained and he showed no signs of slowing down. He was hunched over the bar like a thick turtle, his meaty hands wrapped around the rocks glass that he stared into. Two attractive secretary types came in and looked over at him as they slid onto stools at the far end of the bar. He did not look up and the women shrugged and ignored him. His cell phone rang. Fishing it out of his pocket, he looked at the display then punched it to answer.

He heard on the other end, "Mr. asshole G-man. We need to talk." Tessio was calling directly.

"Who is this and how did you get this number?"

"Oh, I have your number, all right. All you need to know is that I am your worst nightmare. Two days from now at midnight you will be in the Pier 4 Restaurant parking lot. Go to the far corner near the street. Wait there." The call was clicked off like the closing of a coffin lid.

Halloran stared at the phone and thought for a minute. Then he called Hughes. He and Angie were just getting out of the shower when the phone rang. Hughes padded naked and dripping across the apartment to answer his cell phone, which was still in his jacket pocket. Angie dried herself off, then wrapped the towel around her head like a turban and walked back into the bedroom. Hughes watched her round and firm bottom roll as she walked away. "Yeah," he said.

"I got a call. They want to meet," Halloran said.

"Shit. Did you trace it?" Hughes asked, suddenly tense again.

"I won't even try. Those guys are too smart for that and all it would do is raise suspicion at the Bureau."

"What are you going to do?" Hughes's voice was strained. Angie looked out from the bedroom, concerned.

"I have to meet them to see what they know and what they want. I need backup."

Hughes was silent. Halloran said again, "I need backup, partner."

"First of all, I'm not your partner. I'm your patsy. Second, you are pulling me further into where I don't want to go. I'll give you my bag. Throw it at them when you meet and don't contact me again."

"Look, if it's the worst case, we might have to return the money. But, we don't know. They could be just fishing."

"What the fuck are you talking about? You said they've already come to your house. That doesn't sound like fishing. That sounds like caught." Angie went back into the bedroom and shut the door softly.

Halloran said, "Look, you don't have to be seen. Just sit down the street and watch. Get plate numbers, etc. I can give you a signal if I need the posse to come in. You need to know what is going on as much as I do. You've got to do this."

"Jesus, Bill. You talked me into this scheme and my life is sliding away. I just want out. The money's not important and I'll take my lumps on what happened in the motel." Hughes's voice was shaky.

"Don't bail on me now, buddy boy. You can sit in the lot in front of the Institute of Contemporary Art next door and watch through binoculars. Any problems, I'll give you a hand sign. We've got to figure out who these guys are and what they want."

"They want their friggin' money back, is what they want. I'll bring my bag with me and if that will resolve it, I'll throw it out of the car and they can pick it up and leave me alone. All right, Bill, I'll do this one last thing for you and that's it. I hope I never see you again after that."

Halloran's voice softened. "Thanks, buddy boy. I knew you would come through. Day after tomorrow, I'll meet you in the lot in front of the ICA at eleven o'clock. I'll give you the binoculars and show you where you can sit to watch me. See you then."

Hughes hung up. He thought for a minute and shivered. This did not sound good, but he had to know how deep he was in and what might happen. He couldn't let Halloran do this alone. He wouldn't know what was going on.

The next forty-eight hours dragged on like a root canal. The night of the meet was a typical early December evening—a cold northern wind blew swirling snowflakes over the city. Looking out his window at the Common, Hughes felt the chill slice through him like a paper cut. At 10:30, he put on a black pea coat and a knit cap and headed to the Miata, parked a couple of blocks away. A sudden breeze blew grit into his left eye and he had to sit in the car for a couple of minutes before his eye would stop watering. He felt a slight panic knowing he was running late then realized Halloran was doing the smart thing by arriving early. The drive to the Seaport District was only minutes, with the small sports car rumbling along quietly. Turning down Northern Avenue, he pulled into the front of the museum lot, the modern building looming at the edge of the water like some kind of inert alien life form. A crisp wind off the harbor smelled of seawater and algae. He backed the small car into the shadows and turned it off. A soft hum from Boston traffic was the only noise above the crackling of his cooling engine. Then he jumped when the passenger door was abruptly pulled open. Halloran squeezed his heavy frame into the bucket seat. "Glad you made it, buddy boy," he whispered.

"What's going to happen?" Hughes asked.

"Supposedly, they will park in the far corner near the street. You have a good line of sight from here. I don't plan to get out of the car. If anything bad is happening, I will flash my lights twice and you come running." With that, he opened the door, reached down to the ground and pulled in a black trash bag. He took out a Mossberg twenty gauge and laid it across Hughes's lap. Stick this out your window and fire at will. I will be flying out of there. You follow."

Hughes looked at him like he was crazy. "The only thing I would do is fire up in the air. I'm not shooting anybody. You're on your own, buddy boy."

Halloran grinned. "Just cover my ass. My car is parked down the street. I'm going to get it and drive into the Pier 4 lot and back in where you can see me. I'm not getting out of the car. I'll listen to what they say and take off. I'll do some counter surveillance and meet you at O'Malley's. OK?"

Hughes didn't answer as Halloran climbed out of the Miata and disappeared into the dark night. Minutes later, he saw the Lexus pull into the corner of the adjacent lot and back in. Hughes had a clear line of sight. The night closed in around him. He sat uncomfortably in the small car and waited. He could smell the dank harbor some fifty yards away. It looked like shiny asphalt, with occasional white flashes made by the waves.

A half hour later, a large Ford sedan cruised slowly down Northern Avenue. Hughes felt his body tense. This was it. He could see three people in the car, two in front and one in the back seat. It turned into the restaurant lot like a shark gliding toward its prey, and pulled to a stop, nose in, next to Halloran. For two to three agonizing minutes, Hughes could see no movement. Then the back passenger window of the Ford slid down. He saw the side window of Halloran's SUV open, and apparently the conversation began. Hughes pulled the shotgun onto his lap, and felt its cold barrel through his pants. The conversation lasted only five minutes, but it seemed like an hour. Suddenly, the big Lexus lurched forward and sped out of the lot, accelerating toward the now empty financial district. The Ford backed up and eased out of the lot. As it turned onto the street, someone in the front passenger seat stuck his middle finger out the window toward Hughes.

It was almost 11:30 when Hughes parked and walked into O'Malley's. The bar was surprisingly busy and the action reminded Hughes of a time he saw a flock of turkeys going through a mating ritual in a field on Martha's Vineyard. It took him a minute to spy Halloran sitting alone in a corner booth, hunched over and nursing an amber colored drink. He slid in opposite him. "So, Bill, what was that about?" he asked.

Halloran was quiet for a minute then said softly, "They know it was me and somebody else. They spotted you in the parking lot, so now they are looking for a blue Miata. We're in this together." Halloran was sullen.

"Jesus. Who are they?"

"Miami. It was their money and they said they can get help from their customers. That's New York and Boston. Said none of them like to be ripped off by a couple of assholes."

"What do they want?" Hughes looked around to see if anyone was in hearing distance and more specifically, if there was anyone in the bar that might be them.

"What do you think they want? They want their money back. Said they can forget the little elimination of their runner. Said he was just refuse. But the money has got to come back in three days."

"How's that going to happen?"

"No fuckin' idea. He said I would get a text with the time and place," he mumbled.

Hughes looked at him and saw fright oozing off him like fog from a swamp. "Fine. Take mine back and give it to them. It's dirty anyway."

"Not so easy. I've spent about two hundred grand already. And I don't believe them about the hit. I know these guys. The fat guy in back is Sal Tessio. He's Miami. No one fucks with him. It's not like we can go to the FBI or cops."

"That's what you said about them."

"Screw you, buddy boy. Don't think you're not in this too. You're just one small fart from me to you," Halloran hissed.

Hughes stared at him silently. Then he slowly shook his head and said, "I don't care. I just want away from this and you. When I look at you, I realize what's important to me and how much you have compromised my life, but I didn't realize it at the time." He got up to leave. "I'll somehow get my share to you. After that, you're on your own." Hughes stood over Halloran for a brief instant before he turned and strode out of the bar. Halloran watched him go, then swallowed the rest of his drink and signaled for another.

Hughes walked through the cold, dark streets toward his car. Light snow had started to swirl around the streetlights like miniature moths. The chill penetrated him. He started the car and drove slowly the few blocks to Beacon Hill. He had to park inside the Common garage and walk through the park and up the hill to his apartment. Boston Common was deserted except for a bundled-up bum who indifferently shook a cup at him from a bench as he walked by. He let himself in, tossed off his damp jacket, and walked into the bedroom. In the wane and cold light streaming in from the street, he saw Angie curled up in bed. She rolled over, smiled, and held her arms up to him. He sat down on the edge of the bed, leaned over and hugged her. Her warmth was a rekindling of his insides.

"What's new, lover?" she asked.

"They confronted Bill," he said.

"Who?"

"The bad guys."

Angie sat up quickly. Alarmed. "What do they want?" she asked.

"They want all the money back in three days. Said they don't care about the guy Bill shot."

Angie was wide awake now. "So that's good. Give them the money and you're out of it."

Hughes stood and pulled off his shirt and pants. "Don't know. Bill doesn't believe them about forgetting about the shooting and he is more than two hundred thousand short."

Angie was suddenly afraid. "What are you going to do?" she asked.

"I don't know. Right now, the only thing I know to do is hold you." He shed his briefs, slid into bed and did exactly that.

Chapter 42

Angie slowly got out of bed, leaving a heavy breathing Hughes behind. She knew he had slept fitfully because at one point in the middle of the night he got out of bed and stood looking out the window.

She pulled on a heavy cable knit turtleneck sweater and jeans, short boots, and her black pea coat. She left the apartment and walked down to the front foyer of the building. Outside the exterior glass door, the snow seemed to have stopped, leaving a thin white icing on everything. She took her cell phone from her bag and called Laura Halloran. A sleepy and thin voice answered after the sixth ring.

"Laura, it's Angie. I need to see you right away. Is there a place we can meet?"

"What?" Laura said, still half asleep and confused.

"The bad guys are after Bill. Maybe we can head them off if we give them what they want."

"What do they want?" Laura asked, suddenly awake.

"They want their money of course. Do you know where Bill put the money he had?"

"I hid it, but told him where it was. He took it back and put it in the back of his car."

Angie thought for a moment. "Do you think it's still there?"

"I don't know. I really don't think he would bring it back here, especially after those two cretins came to our door. I don't know where else he could put it."

"Jesus, you think he's driving around with it in his car?"

Laura laughed. "Probably. He's a complete jerk now and nothing would surprise me."

"If we could get it and give it back, they may go away. Do you think we could?"

Laura said, "I know where he kept the extra car keys. If they're still here, and we can find the car, maybe we could get it."

"Go look and call me back," Angie said, and hung up. She stepped out onto the irregular sidewalk of Joy Street, now slick with a thin coat of white. She headed up the hill, past the golden dome of the State House and down past the Parker House. Only a few early morning pedestrians were out, bundled thickly against the frosty air. She stopped at Bruegger's Bagels and bought a sesame bagel and coffee. She found a table near the window and watched office workers go by while she waited for Laura's call. Most had their heads down against the cold. Before she finished her bagel, her phone buzzed. "Angie, it's me," Laura sounded excited. "I found them. Now, if we can find his car and he's as stupid as I think he is, we can grab the money and maybe get these guys to go away."

"Where do you think he parks it?" Angie asked, taking the last sip of coffee.

"I'll bet he stuck it in the Bureau parking lot where it would be safe."

"Where's that?" Angie asked.

"Right across from Faneuil Hall. I've been with him a

couple of times when he parked there. It's sort of a special lot for government people. I think we can walk in from the street."

"We've got to do this soon because he's supposed to meet the bad guys in a couple of days."

Laura was excited, either from the anticipated adventure or by the thought of getting even with her husband.

"There's a steak restaurant at the end of Faneuil Hall called Halston's. Meet me at the bar. When can you get there?" Angie looked at her watch. She figured Danny would be up soon and would think she went to work for the lunch shift. "Can you make one o'clock?"

"I'll get there. Meet you at the bar?"

"Good, see you there." Angie hung up and decided to go for a walk. Faneuil Hall was only two blocks away and she could scope out the parking lot Laura had told her about while she was waiting. She buttoned up her coat and stepped out onto the busy sidewalk. She pulled her collar up and turned left on Washington Street, then right onto State. Turning left at the next corner, she scampered across the street and walked along the north side toward the steep stairs leading to city hall. The parking lot was open but inside, she could see a card-activated gate with warning signs indicating that only authorized personnel were allowed. She was sure they could walk around or under the gate, so it was just a matter of finding Halloran's car if it was in there.

Angie crossed the busy street into Faneuil Hall. Even with the cold weather, there were a fair amount of tourists wandering about, taking pictures and window shopping. The unique boutiques that initially populated the store fronts had pretty much given way to national chains, but the tourists still seemed interested. She made her way into the main hall, stopping at Au Bon Pain for another cup of coffee. She carried it into the great hall in the center and sat at a corner table waiting. There were several tourists with cameras, and a school group of chattering ten year olds. A little before one o'clock, she walked up to Halston's. It was located down a short flight of stairs below the walkway. A line of windows looked into the long, rectangular bar, which was mostly filled with young executive types eating lunch. She noticed the usual wine or cocktail glasses were replaced by sodas and Perrier for the lunch hour. She found a seat and the bartender, a trim, dark haired handsome man, came over to her immediately. He smiled warmly and took her order for an un-oaked chardonnay.

He delivered her drink within a minute, smiled and said his name was Randy. She gave back a thin smile and looked beyond him at the television. He walked away.

The wine was very cold and delicious. The second sip calmed her a bit as she thought about the garage only a hundred yards away and what it may contain.

At twenty after one, Laura rushed in. She was wearing a London Fog trench coat tightly belted, and a bright red scarf tied around her neck, but she somehow still looked like a suburbanite. She spotted Angie at the end of the bar, waved and strode over.

"Sorry, I'm late," she said as she pulled off the scarf. "Traffic coming up the expressway was awful." She unbuttoned the coat and slung it over the back of a barstool. She was wearing jeans and a blue t-shirt. She was not wearing a bra, which Randy immediately noticed as he approached. Smiling again, he took her order for the same thing Angie was drinking. The two women looked at each other.

Angie lowered her voice and said, "I walked by the garage. You can walk in, but I don't know what's in there."

"I called his office and the girl said he was there. I left a stupid message and hung up. I figure his car is in the garage. Whether or not what we want is in it is anyone's guess."

"OK, let's have another glass of wine and see what we can come up with. Where's your car?"

"I parked in the lot next door. We have to walk through the marketplace to get to it, but it's only a couple of minutes away."

Angie signaled to the bartender who popped over immediately and gave another smile. Two more glasses of wine arrived and were downed quickly. Angie threw money on the bar and stood up. "Let's go," she said unconvincingly.

The opening to the garage looked like a menacing dark mouth. Looking inside, they could see vague outlines of cars. The two women paused outside, furtively looking up and down the busy sidewalk. No one paid them any attention.

Angie took a deep breath. "Let's go."

Inside was a cavernous space with dozens of cars in neat rows. Many were bland sedans, obviously government issued. Laura led the way, looking for her husband's new Lexus. They stopped suddenly and froze when they heard the slamming of a metal door at the far end. They could see a trim man in a dark suit and white shirt heading for a black Acura parked in the corner. He didn't notice them and drove past as they stood in the shadows. They whispered quietly, walking between the rows. Then Laura pointed and smiled. Looking around, they silently approached the vehicle, which sat resting like a gleaming black opal. They looked in the back and saw some clothes and what looked like a leather shave kit, but no large bags.

Laura looked at Angie and said, "Looks like he's stashed it somewhere else."

"Wait," Angie said. "Can you turn off the alarm and open the back?"

"If these keys work, I can." She pointed the remote toward the car, held her breath and pushed the unlock button. There was a satisfying chirp. Laura grinned at Angie and tried the button for the back hatch. It opened smoothly. Angie stuck her head in, pushed the clothes aside and felt for the spare tire cover. Finding the tab, she pulled it to the side and looked into the tire storage space. No tire, but a black canvas bag.

"Son of a bitch," she muttered as she pulled at it with both hands. "Help me," she said. "It's heavy."

Laura reached inside the car and grabbed a corner of the bag. Together they pulled it out of the car and onto the ground. Excitedly they tried to unzip it, but found it had a padlock on it.

"Let's go," Angie said. Together they hefted the bag back through the garage and out onto the sidewalk. They smiled at each other and started walking, each carrying an end, through the marketplace. Despite the chilly weather, several groups of bundled-up tourists wandered around. None seemed to pay any attention to the two women and their burden. They half-dragged the bag into the garage elevator and up to where Laura had parked. Getting out on the third floor, they looked around and saw no one in sight. Laura opened the back of her Prius and they hefted the bag into the car.

"Let's go to my house," Laura said. "We can open the bag with some tools in the garage."

Together they drove out of the garage and headed to the suburbs. The tension and excitement in the car felt like an electric current. Traffic was flowing and they got to the house in forty minutes. As Laura rounded the corner onto her street, Angie noticed a dark sedan parked along the curb, where every other vehicle was in a driveway.

Without turning her head toward the car, Angie said, "See that? I think I saw a couple of guys in that car."

Laura glanced in the rearview mirror and gasped. "Those may be the guys after Bill. They may be watching to see if he shows up. We'll pull into the garage and close the door before checking out the bag."

Inside the garage, Laura peeked out the window and didn't see anybody. Together they pulled the bag from the car and dropped it on the floor. Laura searched around for something to open it with. She found a large bolt cutter, guided it around the metal and snapped the padlock open. Together they unzipped the bag and peered inside. They looked at each other and smiled.

"OK," Angie said. "If I get Danny's share and give it all back, maybe they will leave us alone."

"How are you going to do that?" Laura nervously whispered.

Angie stood silent. Then she straightened to her full height and took a deep breath. "I'll be damned if I let my and Danny's life together get ruined by this. I've got to take care of it. Do you have any wine in the house?"

Twenty minutes later, with an empty chardonnay glass in front of her, she said, "That's it. I'm going out. Lock the doors behind me." She stood and strode out the front door. She started walking up the leaf covered street, past the well tended lawns and neat looking houses toward the car parked two hundred yards away. She approached the driver's side. Inside the car, the two men were slouched down ignoring her. She knocked on the driver's window. After a couple of seconds, Dino looked up at her and the window slid down with an electric sigh. He said nothing.

Angie said, "I know what you want. I can give it to you. Tell your boss to call me."

She reached into her jeans pocket and pulled out a scrap of paper on which she had written her phone number while drinking the wine. She handed it to Dino who didn't seem fazed and then turned back toward the house. She started walking, cold shivers running up her back. It wasn't until she was back in the house that she dared to look for the car and the two men. It, and they, were gone. Laura was peeking through the blinds and was pale as a ghost. "I can't believe you did that," she said. "Those guys are animals."

"OK," Angie sighed. "You don't have to get involved. You and the kids should stay far away from this. Let's get the bag back in the car and then you can drive me home. I'll put everything together and see if they call."

The ride back to the city was mostly silent and tense. Laura constantly looked in her mirror for a tail, but saw nothing suspicious. Angie had left her Mustang in the Boston Common garage and both women relaxed when they finally arrived there. Laura pulled up behind Angie's car and they lugged the heavy bag from one car to the other. Slamming the trunk closed, and still seeing no one, they smiled at each other and Laura returned to her car without another word. Angie started her short walk up the hill to the apartment.

Chapter 43

She let herself in to the dark apartment and used the cream-colored glow of the street lamps to find her way to the kitchen. She turned on the light and busied herself making coffee. While it brewed, she found the key to the closet in the freezer where she and Hughes had hidden it earlier. She opened the door and looked in. The black bag was still in the back, barely visible. She kicked at it and felt its solid weight. Satisfied the money was still there, she re-locked the closet and poured herself a cup of strong black coffee. She pulled a chair to the window, sat down and put her feet up on the sill. She stared out the window and thought about the next steps. Her resolve increased in tandem with her anxiety.

An hour later, she heard a key in the door and Hughes walked in. Startled to see someone in the apartment, he froze until he realized it was Angie.

"Hi, sport," she said, unconvincingly.

"Jesus, you scared me. These days, all I do is look over my shoulder for something bad."

Angie stood, and walked her coffee cup to the sink. Turning, she gave Hughes a weak smile. "I've got all the money, except for what Bill spent. I'm going to give it back, if they let me."

Hughes was stunned. "You can't even try to do that by yourself. You don't know how dangerous these guys are."

"Danny, we can't go on like this. I will put an end to it if I can. Laura and I were able to get Bill's bag. That dumb shit had it in his car and Laura had a spare set of keys."

"Angie, let's get out of here and talk about this. We need a drink to even think about it."

"Best idea I've heard in a long time." Her smile lit the room. "I'll get my coat."

They walked out into the December chill and down past Chestnut Street's elegant townhouses to Charles Street. Tosca's looked dark and expensive from the street. Walking in, Hughes nodded to the familiar maître d' and they found two barstools at the end of the bar, away from others. Hughes ordered a Jameson for himself and a chardonnay for Angie. When the drinks arrived, they made a small toast to each other and spoke in low tones. The dim light and elegance of the restaurant gave them a cozy closeness.

"Angie, I can't let you do this. It's way too dangerous," Hughes whispered.

"Danny, it's the only way. So far no one except the Hallorans know you are involved. If I can give back the money, maybe this thing will end."

Hughes was silent. They each sipped their drinks and looked at each other.

Angie took another sip and paused. "Danny, I realized over the past few weeks how much I love you. You fucked up royally, but I see you have been suffering from that mistake. That tells me that inside you are a good guy. And I realize that neither of us believes money is the answer to everything. Maybe it's the answer to nothing. If we, and I mean we, can put this behind us, we can move forward and have a good life together. I'll do what I have to do to save you and us."

Hughes was silent. After a minute, he said, "I can't let you do this alone. I'm going with you. I'll sit in the car and watch. You just drop the bags and get right back in and I will get you out of there safely. I can cover the plate on the car and make sure it's really dirty. I'll have my .38 with me."

Angie gave a cynical smile. "I don't know if that's good or bad. Buy me some ziti with meat sauce and we can get comfortable. Seems like it's been years since we got nasty."

"I'll drink to that." And they both did.

An hour later, they headed back up the hill, holding hands. The wind was blowing the light snow around, making it look like shimmering confetti in the gas lamps along the street. They turned the corner onto Joy Street and entered the building. As Hughes unlocked the door to the apartment, Angie's phone started to ring. They looked at each other.

Angie reached into her pocket. "Hello?"

"We want what's ours." The voice was soft and gravely at the same time.

Angie listened intently as they went inside and Hughes locked the door behind them. Twice she tried to reply to what she was hearing, only to be cut off. When she finally clicked the call off and slid the phone into her pocket, she was ashen.

"Tell me what they want," Hughes said.

"They said to meet under the Neponset Bridge tomorrow night at midnight. They said bring all the money and come alone," she said softly.

"Angie, I can't let you do this."

"It's the only way," she said. "They still don't know who you are and they know there was no woman involved in the rip-off. I don't think they would hurt me, not knowing who the other person is, or how I got the money."

"What do you think they will do when they find it short? How much that asshole Bill spent?" Hughes said.

"Nothing we can do about that. I won't give them the money until I get a promise that the whole thing will end." Angie was hopeful.

"Good luck with that," Hughes said. "Well, we have a little more than twenty-four hours to plan this, or to figure out a way to back out. Let's spend this time wisely."

Angie smiled and led him slowly toward the bedroom.

Chapter 44

The next morning, Hughes went down to Charles Street and returned with bagels, cream cheese, jelly donuts, and two large coffees. They spread the food out on the table overlooking the street and ate their breakfast in silence, both deep in thought.

Hughes said, "I know that area. It's smart on their part because they have a bunch of ways to leave. I'll go do a drive-by and figure out our game plan."

Angie stared out the window, again ruminating on the people going about their average lives. "I can't carry both bags, so all I can do is drop them from the car and take off. But I want their promise that this thing is over," she said.

"I'll figure it out. And I have to find a place to sit and watch and be ready to move in if I have to. I think today we need to work out a plan and then rest and be ready to go before midnight. Right now, we have a car sitting in the Boston Common garage with almost six million in cash in the trunk. We have to make sure we have no breakdowns or problems with the plan."

"Danny, I'm scared," Angie was silent for a minute. "But we have to do this. I'll do whatever I have to so we can be normal again. Or, as normal as we can get."

Hughes shrugged. He walked to the window and paused, then said, "OK, I'll be back and we'll figure out a plan." He kissed Angie, picked up his jacket, and went out the door. The Miata was parked on the bottom of Beacon Hill. Hughes brushed off a thin white coating of snow, started it and headed for the expressway. He drove down Arlington Street and started up the ramp for the southbound expressway when his phone rang. He was pretty much sitting on it so it took him a minute to fish it out of his pants.

"Hello."

Dead air for a minute, then, "Where the fuck is my money?" Halloran was in a rage.

"Where you can't get it. We are going to save your ass."

"I gave you yours, now you took mine."

"Listen, Bill. These guys are on to you. We, and I mean you and I, have no choice but to try to get it back and end it. They'll blow you away in a heartbeat."

"I'm a fuckin' federal agent. No one will touch me."

Hughes thought for a minute, then said, "I'll call you back tomorrow." He took a deep breath, ended the call, and turned off his phone.

Within minutes he was at the Neponset off-ramp. He took it and swung to the right toward the bridge, then turned left to get underneath it. He drove through a small, decrepit neighborhood of dilapidated triple-deckers and rundown old cars parked on the street. He looked around at the multiple directions of escape, and noted that all the traffic was above on the bridge ramps, while this area underneath was deserted. He knew why they had picked this spot. He drove through, turned around and went through again. He found a couple of potential spots with a line of sight but it would depend on exactly where the meet would be. If Angie got in any kind of trouble, he thought, he could theoretically drive to her. Hughes was deeply worried about exactly what help he could give, except maybe to get her into the car and away from danger. The last thing he wanted to do was get in some kind of gunfight. Finally, his apprehension a living snake inside him, Hughes made his way back to Boston.

He let himself into the apartment and found Angie just out of the shower, her hair wet and glistening and her skin flushed. He had to smile.

"What do you think?" she asked.

"They've got a good spot for them. All I can think of is for you to get there early and get your car into an exit position. You can then drop the bags and get out of there. I'll be somewhere where I can watch and run interference if I have to."

"I want them to tell me it's over." Angie pulled her towel off and walked into the bedroom to get dressed before he could reply.

"These are not the kind of people you have a nice conversation with," he said. "Just give them the money and get the hell out."

"No way," she said. "We still have to deal with Bill and there's the little matter of their guy getting killed. We have to get some assurance from them that it's over."

"We'll be lucky to escape out of this," Hughes said softly.

Angie shrugged. "We will do what we can. I think we are doing the right thing. I hope Bill will understand that. Let's take a nap so we can be fresh at midnight."

Dusk came slowly. The temperature dropped and an occasional lonely snowflake drifted down. The street lights and gas lights around Beacon Hill came on with a yellow glow, the cold air making soft rings around the lamps. Angie heated soup from cans and Hughes went down to Charles Street, returning with two deli roast beef sandwiches. They each dressed in dark clothes. Angie wore a black turtleneck sweater and jeans under her black pea coat. Hughes pulled on a sweater and found an old dark blue windbreaker not warm enough for being outside but he wanted a good range of motion in the car. They each wore knit caps, his black and Angie's maroon. At eleven o'clock, they headed out. The air was so cold, it seemed to freeze the inside of their nostrils and their breath came out in thick mists. Hughes had parked on Beacon Street, so he got into his car and Angie walked to the Common garage. He stopped outside the exit ramp and waited for her to come out. After a minute, her Mustang convertible exited and slowly turned right onto Beacon Street. Hughes followed behind. He called her phone immediately.

"You OK?" he asked. "Packages still in the trunk?"

She sighed. "Everything is OK. Let's just take it easy. No sense in getting stopped."

They drove in tandem up Beacon, past Joy Street and over the hill to Tremont. Turning left onto Stuart Street in the theatre district, they pulled onto the ramp for the expressway and headed south. Traffic was light, mostly late night commuters. Angie exited at Neponset and swung around underneath the bridge while Hughes kept some distance between them. The few clapboard houses showed no lights and the two working street lights gave off only a marginal glow. The snow started falling harder. Hughes was concerned about leaving tire tracks and that his car windows could get covered. Angie drove into the area and parked under one of the dim street lights. She sat and waited. Hughes did a drive-by, then turned up a side street and tucked his small car behind a fat SUV. He got out and walked back toward where Angie was parked, being careful to stay in the shadows as much as possible. He stopped at the corner and looked for any suspicious vehicles. Angie's Mustang was already showing a thin coat of white on its canvas top. Seeing nothing unusual, he stepped back behind a tree and called her name. She answered immediately, her voice steady and calm.

"See anything?" he asked.

"Nothing. But we're early. I'll sit and wait. Where are you?"

"I can't sit in the car. Too much snow. They'll spot me and I won't be able to get to you fast enough. I'm going to stand where they can't see me and try to be close, but not too close."

"Danny, I don't want them to see you, or figure out who you are. So far, they have no idea about you, only Bill. We have to keep it that way."

"I'll be backup. If you take your cap off, I'll come running. If everything is OK, I'll stay hidden." Hughes shivered.

They waited. The snow kept falling, forming yellow circles around the street lamps, and piling up on the street. Angie had to run her windshield wipers from time to time, and the exhaust fog coming from her car made it easy to spot. Hughes, standing behind the tree, wished he had worn a warmer jacket. He stomped his feet from time to time to try to keep them warm.

Finally, at ten minutes to twelve, a large Ford sedan pulled up and parked halfway down the block from Angie. It sat, menacing in its stillness.

Angie flashed her lights once. Hughes shook snow off

his shoulders and stepped back behind the tree. He pulled the .38 Smith and Wesson from his hip and put it in his jacket pocket. Nothing happened for several more minutes. Then four men emerged from the sedan and started walking slowly toward Angie's car. They cautiously spread out, looking around as they moved forward.

As they got closer, Angie got out of her car and stood in the falling snow, watching them approach. She could feel her heart beating furiously. When the men were fifteen feet away, she said, "I've got your money."

Tessio eyed her warily. Dino was at his side. Angie could see a dark handgun in his right hand. Another man was carrying a shotgun cradled across his chest.

"Who the fuck are you?" Tessio said loudly.

Angie took a deep breath. "I'm just a person that wants to make everything go away." Hughes was watching, still unseen.

"What do you want?" Tessio asked.

Without answering, Angie went behind her car and opened the trunk. She heaved the two bags out, one at a time, and dumped them on the road.

"Here's your money," she said. "Take it and go away. Nothing more will be said or done."

"What about my guy getting offed?" Tessio eyed the bags.

"A mistake. No good will come from chasing that. Let it go. Take your money."

Tessio looked at the other three men. They shrugged. He said to Dino, "Go over there and look at the bags. Make sure the money is there."

He then yelled to Angie, "Step away and let us look at the bags. If my money is there, I'll think about what I'll do."

Angie shivered. Hughes couldn't hear what was being said, but he saw Angie step away from her car and a big man walk toward the bags. He kneeled in the snow, unzipped each and peered into them. He got up, still holding the gun, and looked at Angie. He nodded back to Tessio and moved backward so that he was standing to Angie's side.

Tessio stood, thinking. Finally, he said, "No one cares about that piece of shit. Get in your car and get the fuck out of here. I don't know you and you don't know me. It's too fuckin' cold to discuss this. It's over."

Angie exhaled. She got into her car and slowly drove down the street and into the lighted intersection. She began crying softly with relief. Hughes stood motionless and watched as Tessio gestured to two of the men to pick up the bags. They half-carried, half-dragged them to the sedan and slung them into the trunk. Tessio looked around then stared directly toward Hughes. He smiled, then turned and got into the car, his men following.

When the dark sedan disappeared into the night, Hughes walked back to the Miata and brushed off the windshield. He climbed in and started the car. It responded with a satisfying rumble. He sat for a minute, letting it warm. After a minute, he hit the speed dial on his phone and called Angie.

"You OK?," he said in a whisper.

"I may have to change my pants," she replied, her voice flowing like fresh spring water. He exhaled, and said, "See you back home." He shifted into first and started back to the city. A soft feeling of anxiety mixed with relief swept over him as he pulled onto the expressway.

Chapter 45

T he radio was warning of a snow-related parking ban, so
Hughes pulled into the Common garage and parked on
the second level. He walked up the hill to the apartment,
sliding at times as the snow continued to pile up. He had
his head down against the blowing snow and saw few
other pedestrians. Letting himself in, he saw Angie, still in
damp jeans and turtleneck, making coffee. Few things
looked, felt, or smelled as good.

"Well," she said, turning to him. "What do you think?"

He plopped down onto the couch and kicked off his
soaked Nikes. "Angie, you are fantastic; one tough broad. I
love you. I hope that ends it, but how the hell can we trust
those guys?"

"What are you going to do about Bill?"

"Don't know. He'll be ballistic when he finds out his
money was given back, but I don't quite know what he can
do about it. As he says, who you going to call?"

Angie smiled. "In any event, we should celebrate getting out of tonight alive."

Hughes smiled back. "Let me think of something."

Halloran swung his Lexus into the driveway, almost

taking out the mailbox. His anger boiled with rage. He stormed through the front door, yelling for Laura.

She came down the stairs looking scared. "Bill, please. You'll wake the entire neighborhood."

"Where are the kids?" he asked.

"I sent them to my mom's. I'm in the process of going there, too. The house is yours."

Halloran could barely control himself. "Where the fuck is my money?"

Laura was silent. She backed away, and turned toward the kitchen. "Bill, we had a good life together. That's over. I don't know if it's because of that money or because we've changed. But our kids are more important than each of us, and especially more important than that blood money."

He stared at her. Then with more control and speaking quieter, said, "Where's the money?"

"I gave it to Angie and Danny. I think they were going to return it to try to end this nightmare."

Halloran stood and glared at her. Then he took out his cell phone and hit a speed dial. Hughes answered after the fourth ring.

"You son of a bitch," Halloran hissed into the phone. Hughes was silent.

"I gave you the opportunity of a lifetime and you took my money and screwed me."

"Look, Bill," Hughes's tone was moderate. "You stepped way over the line. And, your so-called foolproof plan blew up in your face. I'm doing what I can to get your ass out of a sling. Not to mention mine."

"Fuck you and your slutty girlfriend and fuck my traitor wife, too." He hung up.

Laura was standing next to the refrigerator watching, shaken and afraid. She couldn't decide whether to run or let the storm pass. Halloran turned and took a step toward her. She sank back against the wall. He glared at her, then turned and strode into the garage. She heard him open the back of the Lexus at the same time that there was a knock at the front door. Laura froze. Then she heard the hydraulic hiss of the rear gate of his car closing. He came back into the kitchen and looked at her. Another knock.

"See who's there," he said. She shook her head. "You bitch. You're worthless." He reached under his jacket and pulled out his Glock, holding it down at his side in his right hand. He went to the front window and tried to see who was standing at the door, but couldn't see anyone. He walked to the door and leaned his ear close, only to jump back as another knock vibrated through the oak. Adjusting his grip on the black weapon, he opened the door three inches and peered through. The silenced .22 long bullet penetrated the middle of his forehead with nothing more than a muffled snap. Halloran fell backward, his eyes staring up, until they glazed over like marbles in seconds. Laura stared from the kitchen in shock. The door stood ajar, but nothing could be seen outside from her vantage point. She stood frozen in place for two long minutes, then ran to the door and slammed it shut, throwing the deadbolt. Trembling all over, she stared down at her husband. She looked out the front window and, seeing no one, returned to the kitchen, sat at the island counter, and sobbed into her hands.

Chapter 46

The next morning was ice cold and clear. A gentle snow had fallen overnight, making the world pristine and pretty. Hughes woke gently, looking over at Angie, who was in a deep sleep. He slid out of bed, pulled on jeans and a turtleneck, and found his leather flight jacket in the same closet that had contained the black bag. He looked down on the floor, half expecting to see it still there. He walked outside to Joy Street, stopped and looked toward the Common. Early risers were striding through the new snow, leaving dark trails behind them. After two deep breaths, he turned, and walked up to Chestnut Street, then down to Charles, occasionally sliding on the brick sidewalk. The 7-Eleven store windows were steamed up, but the bright neon signs inside were still visible. He picked up a Herald and a Globe, and poured two coffees from the coffee bar. Folding the papers under his arm, he headed back up the hill. Sparkling ice crystals were in the air and he slid on the glazed sidewalks. Letting himself into the apartment, he found Angie still in bed. He sat down, smiled at her and waved the coffee under her nose.

"Mmm," she said, sitting up and taking the cup. "How do you feel today after what we did?" she asked.

"I feel like a great weight has been lifted. But it's not over yet. We still have Bill to deal with and what he did and how I'm still mixed up in it. We took the first step. A big step."

Angie took a sip of coffee and smiled. Hughes felt like he was finally home after a long and dangerous trek. He put his coffee down and stretched. He picked up the papers he had tossed to the foot of the bed and started glancing through them. Angie held her coffee in two hands and read over his shoulder. On page three of the Herald, they saw the headline: "FBI agent killed in home accident." They both stopped and stared. They were speechless.

After a moment, Angie said, "Oh my God. Do you think that's Bill? What's Laura going to do?" She paused. "Danny, could it be suicide?"

"Don't know. He was pretty fucked up. Giving the money away may have put him over the edge. The paper says they are treating it as an accident, but not ruling out suicide."

"I'm going to call Laura," Angie said, reaching for her cell phone from the nightstand.

Hughes got up and stood looking out the window at the blowing snow and icy streets. He saw none of that, but was lost in thought about all that had happened. He turned the events over in his mind and decided there was still nothing to tie him directly to Halloran and the heist. But fear sat deep in his stomach like a living demon.

The call went to voicemail and Angie left a message to call her back right away. Laura called within ten minutes.

"Laura, how are you doing?" Angie asked. "What happened?"

There was a pause on the line then Laura said, "It was

them." There was a quiet sob. "I called the police as soon as I knew they were gone and within minutes Bureau agents were swarming all around. They sealed off the house and made me leave. I'm at my mom's with the kids."

"How are you holding up?"

Silence. Then Laura whispered, "He had it coming, the damn fool. Just make sure no one knows anything else."

"I know what you mean," Angie said. "What can we do to help?"

"Nothing right now. I'll call you back later," Laura said and hung up.

"Danny, maybe we should leave town," Angie said, slipping her phone back into her pocket.

"Run away? Where do we go? If they are after us, they will find us." He paced around the apartment while Angie watched him.

"OK, let's think about this," she said. "Is there any way they know you were with Bill?"

"If they tie you to me, maybe." Hughes thought for a minute. "But it would make more sense to them that Bill was with another agent than with someone outside of the Bureau. Maybe they figure killing Bill is an eye for an eye."

"Let's hope. My God, poor Bill."

"Angie, he was heading for something bad. You don't know what an asshole he'd become. He basically abandoned Laura and his kids. He was running with hookers, throwing money around. I don't think I saw him once in the last month where he wasn't at least half drunk."

"Even so, what about Laura and the kids?" Angie shuddered. Then after a minute, she walked over to Hughes, who was standing at the sink splashing water on his face. Coming up behind him, she reached around and held him close. She whispered, "Danny, you made a mistake but then you knew better. I love you even more for what you are going through. It reminds me how good you are inside."

Hughes turned around and looked into her deep, dark brown eyes. They were wet from tiny tears. Putting his arms around her, he said, "Angie, you've stuck with me. Even more, you helped me do the right thing. I hope to God I can get through this and we can go on together. I love you."

The tears flowed stronger from her. "Danny, I love you, too. We'll get through this. Let's go for a walk."

He nodded and they headed for the closet. She pulled on her black pea coat and Hughes put on his weathered leather jacket. They walked down the stairs to the front door, its glass fogged from the cold. Stepping out onto Joy Street, they walked up Beacon to the entrance to the Common, opposite the golden-domed State House. There were few people out. They gingerly made their way along, their footsteps crunching on the icy sidewalks. The air was clear, sharpening the outlines of the high buildings. After a minute, Hughes took Angie's hand in his and they walked in silence in a shared cocoon. The death of Halloran hung painfully in their minds.

Walking across the frozen Common, then across the bridge over the pond in the Public Garden, they turned onto Arlington Street, then onto Boylston Street, stopping at the Parish Café. The heat hit them like a warm blanket as they stepped in from the cold. Angie ordered a latte, Hughes a black coffee, and they sat near the window, quietly watching the Boston winter.

"I'm really sick about this," Angie finally said, almost to herself. Hughes just looked at her and stayed quiet.

"Where do you think we go from here?" Hughes asked.

Angie took a sip of her latte and stared at the swirling snow outside. "I guess we just wait and see. So far, I think only Laura and I know about your involvement. And maybe they're satisfied. They got most of the money back and took revenge. Let's wait and see."

"Angie, I'm still an accessory to murder," Hughes whispered.

"The way I look at it, you were an innocent bystander. You didn't plan to kill anyone and you didn't participate in it."

Hughes stared out the fogged window for a minute. "Let's go home," he finally said.

They walked back through the cold city, carefully walking on the icy sidewalks as they made their way up Beacon Hill. The apartment felt chilly and hollow. Angie made hot chocolate and Hughes found some football on TV. They went to bed early that evening, each alone in their thoughts.

Two days later, the weekend was approaching again. Angie came in from her waitressing shift with a mischievous smile. "OK, Danny, my pal. Nothing seems to be going on, so I made reservations at the Woodstock Inn in Vermont for us."

"What? We can't afford that place."

"Well, we don't have a bag of money, but I have a credit card. I think we deserve it."

Hughes managed a weak smile. "Point me in the right direction. I'll follow you anywhere."

They took Angie's Mustang because the Miata was so awful in the ice and snow. They left Friday afternoon and drove north up Route 95, then cut northwest across New Hampshire at Concord. Then just past White River Junction, they picked up Route 4, and followed it past rolling hills, white as fresh cream. The inn sat back from the road, and had a classic New England regal look. They drove to the front entrance and were met almost immediately by a young man to assist with their luggage. Two smiling young women were at the front desk, welcoming them as they entered. Hughes thought, *if they only knew.*

Their room was modern, yet traditional. A high bed sat against the far wall. They smiled at each other as the bellman placed down their suitcases, explained the thermostat, and mentioned the dining rooms and hours. A light feeling of escape washed over them when the bellman left.

"This is a good idea, Angie," Hughes said. "Maybe I can sleep here."

"I have plans that will help you sleep even better."

The next morning they awoke to a bright and pristine world. They pulled themselves together and headed to the dining room for a buffet breakfast of eggs, home fries, bacon and fruit. Both were famished and Hughes made three trips to the buffet table. After breakfast, they sauntered out into the village that seemed lost in an alternate world of charm. They strolled down cleared sidewalks, the snow piled at the intersections like ice cream cones. They ambled into the galleries and curio shops, looking but not buying. Making their way back, they found an inviting bistro across the street from the inn called Bentley's. They went in for lunch and sat at the empty bar. The bartender, a young man with a winter tan, approached immediately and smiled at the attractive couple.

"How are you folks doing?" he asked by way of a greeting. "I'm Matt."

"We're OK," replied Hughes. "How about a couple of Bloody Marys and a lunch menu?"

"Coming right up." Matt prepared the drinks expertly

and served them on paper napkins. Hughes and Angie took sips and both felt the alcohol go slightly to their heads. They ordered two bowls of onion soup and sipped their drinks slowly.

After a while, Angie said, "I want to talk to Laura. I want to meet with her and see how she's doing. Maybe she has some information for us."

Hughes thought for a minute. "Might be a good idea. Do you think she blames me?"

"How could she? You're the one that got sucked into Bill's scheme. You're the one who gave the money back. And you're the one that tried to talk some sense into Bill."

"Maybe you're right. Do you think I should go with you?"

"I don't know. Maybe just some girl-to-girl talk will help her open up. I think I should try that first."

"Whatever you say."

The weekend flew by. The ride back was easy, but the tension they had escaped started to seep back in the closer they got to Boston. The snow had turned to brown slush from a slight January thaw. The curbs were hard to negotiate and there was still no parking available. Angie pulled the now dirty Mustang into the Common garage and they walked up the hill in silence. It was already dark and the lights along Beacon Street gave off a weak shimmer. The apartment was cold and unwelcoming, but Angie quickly turned on the heat and started the coffee while Hughes sat on the couch and turned on the TV. Despite the returning tension, there was still a comfort between them.

Chapter 47

The next morning, Angie called Laura on her cell phone. It was answered just before Angie was about to hang up. "Hello?" Laura said weakly.

"It's Angie. How are you doing?"

"Hard to figure out. I miss him and I don't. Everything turned upside down so fast."

"I have a nice chardonnay. How about we split it?"

After a pause, "OK. I think I would like that. But, Angie, the kids think it was an accident. I am living like it was. Please respect that."

"Of course. See you in an hour, if that's OK?"

The walkway to the front door was not shoveled and Angie had to step almost on her toes on the uneven path. Laura must have been watching from the door because she opened it before Angie had a chance to knock. Angie had to hide her reaction when she saw Laura's face. It was gaunt and lined, and she looked like she had aged ten years since Angie saw her last.

"Come in," Laura said. "Please don't mind the mess."

"Don't worry about me," Angie said, holding out the bottle of wine. Laura took it and Angie followed her into the kitchen. The house was strewn with dishes and dirty clothes. It was obvious that no one had cleaned for days. Settling in at the kitchen island counter, Laura found two glasses for the wine. With her first sip, she gave a weak smile.

"How are the kids doing?" Angie asked.

"They've been in sort of a shock. I took them out of school for a little while and my mom is watching them mostly." Laura spoke in a monotone.

"Have you seen anyone suspicious around?"

"That's why I sent the kids away. Afraid of those animals. But, I haven't seen any sign of them. Maybe they took their pound of flesh."

Angie drank some of her wine, then got up and retrieved the wine bottle off the counter. She topped off Laura's glass. "Are you OK financially?" she asked.

"I guess so. The Bureau had a large insurance policy, but I keep finding bills that he ran up. He probably figured he had so much money that nothing mattered. Now I'm stuck with a bunch of them. I'll just work through it until it's all behind me." She shrugged.

At the same time, Tessio was watching a dark-skinned young woman in a string bikini mix the Bloody Marys he had demanded. He grunted when she bent over to pick up a napkin she dropped. Across from him, Dino sprawled out on the flowered couch reading a *Sport's Illustrated* magazine. He sat upright as the woman headed to him with the tray of drinks. He took one, leered at her, and took a sip. "So, big man, what's next? How's New York and Boston?"

Tessio took his eyes off the woman and answered. "They never gave a shit about us losing the money. They probably figured it was funny, but they probably gave us credit for getting it back."

Outside, the winter Florida sun created sparkling diamonds on the Intercoastal just one hundred feet away. Two other women, both topless, lounged at the pool. Dino looked outside at the scene and mumbled, "Life is good." Then he asked, "What about the other guy. The guy we figured was not the shooter?"

"The way I figure it, it must have been another Fed." Tessio said. "We got away with snuffing one federal agent. I'm not going to push my luck. As far as I can figure, whoever the guy is, he's laying low. The Bureau is covering its ass, calling it an accident. That's fine with me."

"So, no more trips up north?"

"Too fuckin cold and no point. Go to the track and enjoy yourself. I give you the week off."

Dino looked at Tessio and slowly finished his drink, holding his glass out for a refill. He smiled.

In her kitchen, Laura fiddled with the buttons on her cotton blouse. They had finished the wine that Angie brought. Outside, brilliant sunshine sparkled off the snow covered lawn. Inside, dry heat filled the kitchen.

"I think there's another bottle in the fridge," Laura said, getting up. Angie could not believe how much weight she seemed to have lost so fast.

Laura found another bottle of chardonnay and opened it with a corkscrew she found in a drawer. She poured a large glass for herself. Angie waved off more.

"When everything gets settled, I think I will sell this place and maybe move closer to the city. I'll look for a district with good schools," she mused, almost to herself.

"What do you think about Danny?" Angie asked.

"I think he's a good guy. Bill sucked him into his get

rich quick scheme. I don't blame him for anything that happened."

"It's been eating at him," Angie said. "Not only what happened but what may still happen. He feels he was part of a crime. I think he's scared about going to jail for the killing."

"I don't know what happened that night, but I can't imagine Danny doing anything bad, other than agreeing to Bill's stupid plan. I'll bet Danny agreed more out of loyalty to Bill than anything else," Laura said.

"It's been so weird since it happened. In some ways, we've gotten closer. Other times, he's so distant it's like I don't know him."

Laura stared at Angie for a minute, thinking about the time with Danny in her house. Then she said, "Angie, he's a quality guy. Bill, for all his bluster and macho crap, I think was really weak. When he got that money, his true personality came out. He couldn't handle it. He never considered who he was hurting, including Danny and even himself."

Angie shrugged, pondering what Laura was saying. Then she said, "I wish it all could end, but I don't know how."

"Hopefully, the mob has let it go. Now he has to deal with the law, but I can't imagine that they care about a dead mob guy. All I know is that Danny and you should be able to go on with your lives."

"I think I will have a little more wine," Angie said. Laura poured half a glass for her, and gave a weak smile. "Do you think he should turn himself in?" Angie asked.

"If that's the only thing that will get it off his back. Somehow, he's got to get closure."

They were silent for a few minutes, each sipping their

wine. Then Angie reached over and put her hand on Laura's. "Take care of your kids. I appreciate everything you said. I've got to shove off, but I'll stay in touch. If you need anything, please call me."

"Thanks, Angie. It's amazing how much and how fast things have changed with one act of greed and stupidity."

Angie stood and walked to the sink to rinse out her glass. Laura sat, looking like an aging librarian instead of the hot suburban wife of only months ago. Angie leaned over, gave her a kiss on her cheek, and headed out the door. As she drove her Mustang through thick traffic back into the city, she thought about what Laura said. As an early and frigid night swallowed up the city, she resolved to save Danny by doing the right thing.

Chapter 48

D anny didn't ask her about Laura when she got home. He seemed like he was putting the situation into a closed box. He made spaghetti and they ate in strained silence, both consumed with their own thoughts. They cleaned up together in a standard domestic dance.

The next week went by in a haze. Angie worked two doubles and Hughes got a divorce case that required intensive surveillance. Getting back into a routine seemed to help alleviate the tension. As January closed out with a minor flaw, Angie felt closed in.

"Let's go a walk," she said, on a rare day off. "The sun seems to be warming up."

Hughes was sitting at his small desk sorting surveillance photos. He was drawn and pale. He looked over at Angie and worked up a smile. "OK, I can't seem to concentrate, anyway. Maybe fresh air will help."

He pushed aside his work and stood up. He had lost ten pounds over the last month and it showed. Angie looked at him with sympathy. They hadn't made love in days. Hughes seemed uninterested. Pulling on their winter jackets and hats, they made their way down the stairs and out the front door to the sidewalk, now fringed with gritty and dirty snow.

"Where to?" Hughes asked.

"Let's head across the Common and down Commonwealth. I love the trees and lights there," she replied. He shrugged and they headed off. While the sidewalks were clumped with dirty snow and difficult to converse, the promenade on Commonwealth was still winter pristine. They strolled down the middle walkway, all the way to the poignant statue honoring the firemen that died in the Vendome fire. Angie took Hughes's hand as they silently strolled. After some minutes, Angie said she was getting a chill and suggested they swing over to Boylston and stop at the Starbucks there. "They have great hot chocolate," she said.

Starbucks was busy as usual, laptops on all the tables and people killing time on the couches. They stood in line for the drinks, and found a small table in the back to sit.

Angie held her hot chocolate cup with both hands and inhaled its heat. "Mmmm," she whispered. Hughes got his usual black coffee and sipped at it with caution.

Both were quiet. Then Angie said seriously, "Danny, I have something on my mind." He looked up expectantly.

"You are carrying something bad inside. I think you have to do something to get closure."

He looked at her for a minute, then said, "What would you suggest? I'm an accessory to murder if the Bureau comes after me and I still don't know if there is a contract out on me from the mob."

"I don't think we can do anything about the bad guys, but chances are they have no idea who you are. Was there anything to link you to Bill with those guys?"

Hughes thought for a minute. The low hum of conversations resonated throughout the coffee shop, and a cold, piercing wind blew in each time a customer entered. "I can't think of any way they could know, unless Bill said something. But I doubt he would have done that. He was too street smart."

"OK, then we have to worry about legal stuff," she said. They were both silent. Then, "What about turning yourself in?"

Hughes looked her aghast. "What? Go to jail?" he said, a little too loud.

Angie looked around and saw no one paying attention to them. She whispered back, "Danny, how long can you go on worrying? Isn't it better to get it behind you one way or the other?"

After a minute, he said, "You're right. I did a stupid thing and unless I get it behind me, I'll be living in fear, not to mention, guilt. Angie, you're the best. You've stood by me throughout this mess and haven't run away, screaming. I'll figure out how to do that."

Back at the apartment, Angie went to the refrigerator and pulled out a bottle of St. Ives chardonnay. She poured two glasses while Hughes prepared some chicken thighs, dipping them in beaten egg and cornmeal. He laid them on a greased tin and put them in the oven. The windows were soon covered with a thin fog as the apartment got warm and cozy. The wine was crisp and cold, the chicken hot and delicious. They ate in silence, Angie only occasionally saying how content she suddenly felt. When the wine was gone, Hughes took her by her hand and stood her up. She smiled as he led her into the bedroom.

Hughes woke from an unusually deep sleep and reached over to find Angie gone. He found her in the kitchen, wearing one of his oxford shirts, mixing batter for corn bread. She already had a half dozen eggs beaten and set aside, ready for the pan. He smiled and hugged her from behind.

"Morning, sleepyhead," she said, over her shoulder.

"Morning. This is a treat."

"This is an important day and we need as much strength as we can get."

"Important?"

Turning around to him, she said, "Like we talked about last night. We have to go to the Bureau and face it."

He was quiet. After a minute, he said, "You're right. Got to do that. There's nothing in the future if we don't close this up. I'm ready."

They ate in silence and dressed for the cold and frosty day. The FBI headquarters in Boston comprised several floors in a typical government building—massive and impersonal, its imposing girth overlooking the color and frivolity of Faneuil Hall. Hughes and Angie walked into the reception area, each knowing they were making an irreversible passage in their lives. As they started across the weathered linoleum floor, Hughes turned to Angie and looked deeply into her eyes. "You are not part of this. I am. Wait here."

"No, Dan, I want to stay at your side."

"This is the one thing I have to do by myself and for myself. I was part of a horrific incident; you just had the misfortune of knowing me. Please, Angie. You've done too much already. I will not let you get any more sucked into this nightmare."

Angie looked at him with tears in her eyes. "Dan, let me."

"No," he cut her off. "Without you I probably wouldn't even be here. You've done more than enough." With that he turned and walked the last fifteen feet to the reception-ist, who was watching with interest. "I need to speak to SAC Kenny," he said quietly.

She looked at him with suspicion. "What's your busi-ness?" was her curt and businesslike response.

"I need to talk to him about a murder"

"Is this FBI business?"

Hughes straightened up. "It involves a former agent," he said.

"Take a seat," she said, gesturing to a leatherette couch in the far corner. She tapped something into her computer and turned back to the original papers she was sorting.

Hughes went back to Angie, who was standing by the entrance.

"Please go. I need to do this myself," he said to her.

"I'll go to O'Malley's and wait for you there. Good luck. I love you." With that, she leaned up and gave him a kiss on the lips, spun around and strode out the door, her footsteps clacking as she disappeared down the hall. Hughes sat down and waited. He ignored the out-of-date magazines lying on the table next to him. Thirty-five long minutes later, a trim and groomed young man, dressed in gray slacks, white shirt, and striped tie, came out from the inner offices. He stood just inside the reception area and looked around. Then he gestured to Hughes to follow him through the door. Hughes felt like he was stepping off the edge of a cliff.

He followed the man down a hall with a series of num-bered doors until they came to Agent Kenny's office. The young man knocked lightly and opened it, nodding to Hughes to enter. He walked in and found an oversized desk, guarded on each side by a flagpole, one American, the other Hughes assumed was the Bureau flag. Behind the desk, looking down at some papers, was Special Agent in Charge Craig Kenny. He was a large man, with massive shoulders and a square face. His thick brown hair was neatly combed and parted on the side. His white shirt was rolled up at the sleeves displaying muscular forearms. He nodded to one of the two wooden armchairs in front of his desk for Hughes to sit. He continued to look down and read, occasionally making pencil marks on the document. Finally, he looked up. "Ok, why are you here?"

"I know about and was involved in the reason Bill Halloran got killed," Hughes said, as clearly as he could.

The FBI SAC stared at him. He stood up and turned toward the window behind his desk. Outside, despite the chilly weather, Faneuil Hall was throbbing with tourists and lunching office workers. He stood quietly for a minute, then turned back.

"Bill Halloran was a good and dedicated agent of the FBI. He was killed accidently when his gun went off while he was cleaning it. There is not anything more to that story. As to the rumor of mob money stolen by persons unknown, our confidential sources indicate that, even if true, it's old news and doesn't concern the Justice Department." He turned back and stared at Hughes.

"I want to turn myself in," Hughes whispered.

"Turn yourself in for what? Trying to besmirch the reputation of a good agent? Starting something that the media can make a sensation out of? Get the fuck out of my office. There is nothing about this that concerns you. Get the fuck out before I yank your license."

Hughes stood up, stunned. "You know who I am?"

Agent Kenny bore down on Hughes. "Of course I know who you are. Get out!"

Hughes turned and headed out the door. Standing

outside was the same agent that had led him in. He nodded to Hughes and led him back down the hall and into the reception area. The receptionist did not bother to look up at him as he walked out the door. The air outside felt as clear as vodka and as intoxicating. He walked in a daze, rolling over in his mind the last ten minutes. Finally, halfway down Devonshire Street, he pushed open the front door of O'Malley's. Across the room seated on a barstool, Angie sat with fear in her eyes. Her legs were crossed and her skirt was pulled high, her long legs facing him. He never saw anything so beautiful. He managed a silly smile.

"How's it going, killer?" Angie said with some hesitation.

"He wanted no part of me. They're staying with the story that Bill's death was an accident. I can't even turn myself in."

"What a shock. The FBI wants no dirty skirts. So, does this mean their case is closed?"

Hughes thought for a minute. "I guess so. If Bill's death is closed out as an accident, they can't be investigating the killing. So I guess that case is closed, unless NYPD investigates, but I doubt that will ever happen if the Bureau wants nothing to do with it."

Angie signaled the bartender and ordered a Black Bus Irish whiskey, neat, for Hughes. Her smile turned into a grin. "And, only me and Laura even know you were there. She is surely not going to say anything. The last time I talked to her, all she wanted to do was close that chapter of her life. So, I guess, honey bunch, we should close it also."

Hughes shrugged then smiled as well. Finally, he said, "It will take me some time to forget everything. Some private eye, huh? Without you, I don't know where I'd be."

"I think you're the best private eye there is. You can be tough, but you've got a conscience. And some other things that get attention."

Hughes took a sip of his drink and shivered. He looked into Angie's dark brown eyes, then glanced around at the bar that was now filling with attractive and seemingly care-free office workers. Already he was getting past it.

"I had a feeling everything would work out. I didn't know how, but I figured it would. So, while sitting here fending off some horny guys, I got an idea." She fished into her shoulder bag and pulled out a brochure for Key West. "How about we do some personal investigating someplace away from this cold city?" She uncrossed and re-crossed her legs.

"Thank God for you, Angie."

Outside, the tired old city pulsed on.

END